The Incident at Sunny Banks

by

Kay Pritchett

Mosey Frye Mysteries, Book 5

The Incident at Sunny Banks

Cover Art by *Kristian Norris*

The Wild Rose Press, Inc.
PO Box 708
Adams Basin, NY 14410-0708
Visit us at www.thewildrosepress.com

Publishing History
First Edition, 2023
Trade Paperback ISBN 978-1-5092-5039-4
Digital ISBN 978-1-5092-5040-0

Mosey Frye Mysteries, Book 5
Published in the United States of America

"You know, something else has been bugging me," Olivera said.

"What's that?" McGinnis asked.

"Lauren Wilson."

McGinnis didn't respond, just wrinkled her nose.

"How did she know about Sunny Banks?" he continued. "Technically, it wasn't on the market. She came from Philadelphia to see it. She looked at a couple of other houses, but according to Ms. Frye, this was the one she wanted."

"Maybe she heard about it when she came for her interview."

"Yes, must have. I ought to call Ms. Frye, see what she knows about that. By the way, Carlotta said she didn't think John Doe here had a memorable face."

She moved back to the gurney and lifted the sheet. "He has a handsome face. Youngish, pleasant, but I'd agree. No distinguishing features except maybe his teeth."

Curiosity piqued, Olivera approached the gurney. "What about his teeth?"

She slipped on gloves and pulled back the victim's lips. He had perfectly straight teeth but with unusually pointed cuspids. "Not many people have that. Otherwise, he has a fine set of teeth, not a single filling."

Olivera lowered his brow. "You aren't suggesting he's from a long line of vampires, are you?"

"No, silly." She laughed.

"Whew. That's a relief. Okay, Mr. John Doe, who are you? It's as if you didn't want us to know. No ID, a handsome face but no distinguishing characteristics except a couple of spiky canines. Hmm. Nobody around here knows you. I wonder if Jack Eldridge knows you. He should, you were in his father's car." He looked at McGinnis. "I guess I'm going to Vicksburg."

Praise for Kay Pritchett

"The first in the Mosey Frye Mystery Series, *Murder in High Cotton* by Greenville native and former University of Arkansas professor, Kay Pritchett, is a true page-turner, keeping the reader in suspense. 'Delta folk ought to read *Murder in High Cotton*,' the Fayetteville author jokes, 'if for no other reason than to see if they figure as the culprit or the victim.' Pritchett's foray into the mystery genre, after publishing three academic volumes, must be deemed a success."

~ *Jack Criss of Delta Magazine, an editorial review*

Dedication

For Dianne, Bill, Lennie, and Elizabeth

Other Wild Rose Press Titles by Kay Pritchett

*Murder in High Cotton: The Mosey Frye
Mysteries, Books 1 - 3*

*The Summer House at Larkspur: The Mosey Frye
Mysteries, Book 4*

Chapter One

It was the second of November, All Souls Day, and Mosey Frye was walking over to Abboud Antiques to help her friend Nadia empty the display window of Halloween decorations. But passing the entrance to her daddy's old law firm, she succumbed to curiosity and climbed the stairs to Frye, Frye, and Humphrey, thinking she'd have a quick chat with her step-aunt Carlotta, or, if not her, Dot Cowsley, secretary to a long line of Fryes. Mosey had a question about Waite House, even though the murder of its owner Delaney Crump had long been solved. Her daddy's admonition, *Stay away from Waite House, ya hear?*, still reverberated in her ears—uncannily, mind you, for Ellis Frye had been dead some eight years.

Back around January, not long after Mosey had listed Waite House, she'd spoken with Dot about Ellis's misgivings. Dot didn't disappoint. Didn't spill the beans entirely, no, but gave Mosey enough to whet her appetite. Must have been one of those situations—what'd her psych prof call it? *Cognitive dissonance?* Yeah, that was it. Dot clearly *wanted* her to know the full story behind Ellis's clash with the Waites but somehow felt conflicted, torn, maybe, between her loyalty to him

1

and… "If not Old Man Waite," Mosey muttered, "then for heaven's sake who?"

She reached the top of the stairs and peeped through the glass. The lights were out. She idled on the landing for a second but, needing to get to Nadia's, gave up and went on her way.

Her ruminations carried her around the Square and down Lee Street to the store. She paused outside the entrance and waved to Nadia. Inside the display and completely surrounded by Halloween paraphernalia, Nadia looked just like a witch—ha!—her eyes twinkling through a veil of long, dark hair.

Mosey pushed through the door.

"What took you so long?" Nadia held out a couple of ceramic pumpkins.

"I stopped by the law office," Mosey said, "but no more than a minute—nobody was there." She took the pumpkins from Nadia and, finding a cloth on the counter, gave them a good wipe. "I don't like seeing these things packed away." She sighed and set them in a cardboard box.

Nadia stepped out of the window. "What's wrong?"

"Huh?"

"You sighed."

"Nothing. A girl can't sigh?"

"Pack those pumpkins tight with newspaper. I don't want any breakage."

Mosey crumpled up some pages from an old *Gazette*, and as she was stuffing them into the corners, a blotchy ball of fur alighted at her side. "Qittah, where'd you come from?" Nadia's cat had spung up on the counter and was pawing at the edge of the box.

"You didn't really answer me," Nadia said.

"If you must know, it's something Dot Cowsley said…long time ago." She lifted Qittah from the counter to the floor. "Can't get it out of my head."

"What'd she tell you?" Nadia dragged a scarecrow as tall as she was out of the window, propped it against a Louis Quinze carved settee, and stepped back in.

"Remember when we were kids," Mosey said, "and we'd go trick-or-treating? Every year without fail, Daddy'd tell me to stay away from Waite House."

"A lot of good it did." Nadia chuckled.

Mosey wedged a ruffle of cardboard between the pumpkins and went on with her story. "So, I started wondering about that when I listed the house. Gosh, it's been almost a year."

"Why are you thinking about that now?"

"Halloween, I suppose."

"What's Halloween got to do with it?"

Mosey sighed again, this time with exasperation. "Trick-or-treat. Waite House. Are you listening to me?"

"Yes, for pity's sake, I'm listening."

"So—" Mosey batted her eyes. "—as I was saying, I dropped by the law firm, back in the spring, thinking I'd see if Carlotta or Dot knew anything about that—us and the Waites—but Carlotta wasn't there, and Dot said, no matter, Carlotta wouldn't know anyway."

"She wasn't even around when we were kids," Nadia said.

"True. She and her mom didn't move to Hembree till— Well, let's see. I was still single when Granddaddy married her mom." Mosey ticked off the years on her fingers. "Twelve or thirteen years ago, give or take a little. But what I was thinking was family lore and all that. Being older, Carlotta might have had an inkling."

"So, you asked Dot. And?"

"She opened right up, sort of like she wanted me to know or was dying to tell *somebody.* You know Dot."

"Not someone I would confide in." Nadia stepped out of the window holding a wrought-iron candelabra and set it next to the scarecrow.

"I don't know about that." Mosey crumpled up another page of the newspaper. "Dot's a sweetheart."

"I didn't say she wasn't, but she loves to gossip."

"She's not the only one." Mosey rolled her eyes toward Nadia.

Ignoring the insinuation, Nadia said, "What'd Dot say?"

"Don't tell anybody this."

"Cross my heart."

"Back when Daddy was in law school, he sort of had a thing going with Mona, the Waites' youngest daughter—"

"Interesting."

"—till she suddenly disappeared."

Eyebrows lifted, Nadia faced Mosey. "Mona disappeared?"

"For months, and it all started one night when she was supposed to meet Daddy at the Tavernette, which is why Old Man Waite blamed *him* for her disappearance."

"If he had a bone to pick with Bud, that'd be reason enough to tell you to stay away from there. Did she ever come back?" Nadia stepped in the window again and emerged with a pair of black crystal cachepots.

"She did, but months later."

"Ha," Nadia said, setting the pots on the counter, "you know what that sounds like."

"Yes, I do." Mosey ran her cloth over the cachepots.

4

"You want these in bubble wrap?"

"Yes, and be careful."

"I wouldn't think of breaking your precious planters—that's what they are, aren't they?"

"Not sure I'd stick a plant in one of those."

Mosey rolled the cachepot over in her hand. "Dang! Who in Hembree blows that much money on a little ole piece of black glass? Four hundred and forty-nine bucks?"

"No one, obviously."

"Is that for just one?"

"I'd take eight hundred for the two."

Mosey breathed deep, reached for more bubble wrap, and tucked it around the cachepots.

"She didn't bring it back with her?" Nadia asked, then added, "the baby, I mean."

"No, and mind you, Dot didn't *say* she was pregnant. She didn't say that. But it was hard not to infer—"

"Maybe she *wasn't* pregnant, maybe she just wanted to get out of the house. You don't happen to know what she told your daddy before she left."

"Didn't tell him anything. According to Dot, she stood him up." Mosey topped off the cachepots with a layer of newspaper, then flopped down on the settee and stretched out her legs. "He went to the Tavernette, waited and waited. And when he found out she'd left town, he looked high and low, called Fayetteville to check with their friends at the university. Nobody knew a thing, or so they said. Then out of the blue, Mona's parents got a postcard from California."

"California! She didn't have to go that dang far to find a home for unwed mothers."

"Yeah, Memphis is certainly a lot closer." Mosey absentmindedly pulled a piece of straw out of the scarecrow's burlap sleeve. "That's where most girls went back then."

"Would you stop that," Nadia said. "Look at the mess you're making."

Mosey looked down at the floor, where the piece she'd distractedly removed had let loose an entire sleeve's worth of straw. "Nadia, you are obsessed with neatness." She stood up. "Hand me the broom."

"Never mind. I'll sweep it up later."

Mosey flopped back down. "You want to hear the end of this or not?"

"Yes, but stop fidgeting and get to the point."

"Yes, ma'am." Mosey gave a salute, at which Nadia flashed her an icy stare. "So, some months later—"

"—like nine?"

"I don't know if it was nine or six or who cares, but Mona came home, and according to Dot, that was the end of it."

"Not quite," Nadia said.

"What do you mean 'not quite'?"

"Well, not if your daddy kept insisting you keep away from there."

"Yeah," Mosey nodded. "And that's exactly why I asked Dot in the first place." She rested her head against the settee and looked up at the ceiling. "Why, after all those years…?"

"You'd think, with Mona gone from here—"

"I know," Mosey cut in. "I never even met the woman. Did you?"

"Never had the pleasure."

"Whatever happened must have left a bad taste in

Daddy's mouth."

"Huh!" Nadia blurted. "More than a bad taste."

"But he never said a word about it, not once. And I must have asked a dozen times. All he'd say was, 'Never you mind,' " she drawled, dropping her voice an octave, " 'Stay away from there, ya here?' Remember how he talked in that low, slow voice?"

Nadia nodded and smiled.

"You know something?" Mosey said.

"What?"

It seemed the perfect moment to reveal her long-kept secret. "Promise you won't laugh?"

"Well, I might, if I can't help myself."

"You're going to think I've lost my feeble mind." She squinted one eye, as she often did when she was about to say what she didn't feel comfortable saying. "I hear Daddy sometimes."

"What do you mean you *hear* him?" Nadia, about to wrap a crouching black panther, set it down with a thump.

"I hear him," she stressed, "like I'm hearing you."

"Yeah, right." Nadia picked up the panther and flicked off a piece of lint.

"I mean it. I hear him clear as day."

"Mosey, don't be ridiculous."

"I'm *not* being ridiculous." She shouldn't have told her. She knew she wouldn't believe her.

"Well, what in heaven's name does he say?"

"The same stuff he's always said, like 'Stay away from Waite House.' "

"Which you've consistently ignored." Nadia wrapped the panther in layers of tissue and set it back on the counter.

7

"Well, yeah," Mosey said. "What was I going to tell my boss? That Ellis Frye, dead as a doornail, didn't think it was such a great idea? That house was worth a bundle."

Nadia laughed.

"And not so long ago, when I was out at Larkspur," Mosey leaned forward, "he kept telling me to get the heck out of there—and other stuff."

"What *other* stuff?"

"I don't remember exactly. Warnings about this and that."

"Do you ever tell *him* anything?"

"Course I do. It's like a conversation."

"Girl, I'm worried about you."

"Nothing to worry about. It's not like he's gonna *do* anything."

"I know he wouldn't *do* anything." She lowered the panther into the box, laid a newspaper on top, and closed the flaps. "Does Robert know?"

"Good heavens, no." Mosey stood and checked her watch. "And don't you tell him."

"Where're you going? You just got here."

"Sorry, I've got a client coming at ten thirty. And don't touch that," she said, shoving the half-full box with her foot. "I'll finish when I get back."

"Who are you meeting? Anybody I know?"

"Nope, but I'll introduce you when she gets here. Hugh's picking her up in Little Rock."

"A friend of Hugh's?"

As Mosey anticipated, her mention of a woman in connection with Hugh Jessup piqued Nadia's curiosity. "Sort of," she said. "She's the new hire in Psychology."

"But Hugh's in Anthropology. Why'd he go?"

"You wouldn't be jealous, would you?" Mosey

teased.

"No, fool."

"Well, since you're interested, he and Robert were on the hiring committee."

"What's her name?" Nadia asked coolly.

"Lauren Wilson. I hear she's a knockout."

Nadia threw an owl-shaped needlepoint pillow at Mosey's head.

Mosey dodged the pillow, but Qittah did not.

"Mrrow!" He leapt into the air and skittered under the settee.

"Poor thing," Mosey said to Qittah. "Did she scare you? She scared me, too."

"Get out of here."

Mosey grabbed her jacket. "I'll be back soon as I can." She gestured toward the box as she closed the door, mouthing through the glass, "Don't touch that."

Chapter Two

November 2, 10:00 a.m.
Shepherd Realty

Mosey climbed in her old pickup and hightailed it around the corner to Shepherd Realty. She skidded into her parking place next to Saffron Smiley's new muscle car and cleared the front door at a run. She was halfway to her office when Saffron shouted, "Hey, you going to a fire?"

"I hope not," Mosey yelled back.

It was Saffron's job to keep the business running, which meant tracking down John Earle Shepherd, the absentee owner, and keeping an eye on Mosey, the company's sole agent. Saffron looked and dressed like a real estate agent but seldom exhibited any real enthusiasm for selling houses. But Mosey didn't fault her that. It would have been purely hypocritical if she had.

"Hugh called," Saffron yelled as Mosey disappeared into her office. "The plane was a little late."

"All that racing around for nothing," Mosey huffed as she returned to reception. "When are they getting here?"

"Soon, depending on traffic." Saffron laid down the newspaper. "Where you been?"

"Over at Nadia's, packing up Halloween stuff."

"She's not having an after-Halloween sale?"

"Nope, she's putting it all in storage."

"Well, I swanny." She tossed her pen on the desk. "Thought I might pick up some cheap whatnots."

"You decorate for Halloween?"

"Well, of course. You think Black folks don't celebrate?"

"No, I didn't say that, but I thought—"

"—that we were all scaredy-cats?"

Mosey giggled. "No, silly."

"Uh-huh—" She toggled her head. "—you got some old-fashioned ideas, Mosey Frye. You know that?"

"Hey, listen," Mosey said. "I don't guess you've heard from John Earle this morning."

"He called a little while ago. Why?"

"I'm wondering how I ought to approach this appointment. The house Lauren saw on the Hembree website isn't on the market yet but might be any day."

"Which one's that?"

"The Eldridges' place off Little Smith."

Saffron frowned. "Not sure I'd show her that."

"Why? It's exactly what she wants. A fixer-upper, a big front porch—"

"Why in tarnation does everybody want a big front porch?" She made a face and waved her long, graceful fingers in the air.

"Heck if I know. Fashionable, I suppose."

"When does she need it?"

"I don't know," Mosey said. "She starts teaching in the spring, but if she buys a fixer-upper, she'll need to find a contractor right away."

At the squeak of car brakes, Mosey leaned toward the window. "That's them."

Saffron squeezed out of her niche and joined Mosey

at the window. "Check out Hugh opening the door for her."

"So, what do I say about the Eldridge house?" Mosey said.

"Tell her about it." Saffron returned to her chair. "But tell her it's not on the market yet. Give her some other options."

The door opened and in came Lauren, with Hugh right behind.

"Hi, Hugh," Mosey said, then turned to Lauren. "I'm Mosey Frye, Robert Ellison's wife. We talked on the phone last week."

"This is Dr. Lauren Wilson," Hugh said.

"Lauren," she corrected, shaking Mosey's hand, "call me Lauren. I appreciate your seeing me on short notice."

"Not at all. Glad to help. This is Saffron Smiley."

Saffron stood and nodded at Lauren. "Nice to meet you. Here's a brochure. It's got our phone numbers, should you want to get in touch."

Hugh checked his watch and took a step toward the door. "Ladies, sorry, but I need to get back to campus. I could be available after three, if you need me."

"I'll text you, okay?" Mosey said, waving goodbye to Hugh. "Let's go in here," she said to Lauren as she led the way down the hall. "I have a whole bunch of houses I want you to see."

"You ladies want coffee?" Saffron called out.

"Thanks, I'd love a cup," Lauren said.

Saffron headed for the coffee niche. "I'll make y'all a fresh pot. Is regular okay?"

"Yes, please." Lauren followed Mosey into her office. "That's a beautiful desk, looks like an antique."

"It is. They were about to chuck it out over at the law firm—my daddy's old firm—and I claimed it. Have a seat. May I take your coat?"

"That's okay." She slipped out of her coat, a plain gray cashmere with pearl buttons, and tossed it over the back of the chair. "I thought it'd be cold here, but I guess not."

She wasn't a knockout, as Mosey had told Nadia—for no reason other than to get her goat. But she did have a pleasant appearance with pretty brown eyes and dark ginger hair that hung from a middle part past her shoulders.

"This time of year, it's hard to know about the weather," Mosey said. "We could be in wool sweaters or sleeveless dresses. Where are you from, by the way?"

"Philadelphia," Lauren said as she sank into a leather armchair.

"Oh, wow, you did come a piece. But you've been here before, right?"

"For the interview, but that was in June, and I wasn't here more than a couple of days."

"I remember." Mosey sat in her upholstered swivel. "We had an appointment, but you had to cancel."

"I'm sorry about that, but it wouldn't have worked out."

"Oh?"

"I didn't really have time to see any houses."

"Well, you're here now, and I'm sure we'll find something for you." Either that or pitch a tent. Mosey crossed her legs. "Are you still thinking in terms of a fixer-upper? You mentioned that in your message."

"Yes, I love older homes. Don't care much for these new places, gray walls, wide-open spaces."

13

"You've come to the right place, then. I don't think Hembree has anything like that, not yet. We're sort of on the periphery of the fashion world." She placed a picture of the Eldridge house on the desk in front of Lauren. "So, we talked about this one." She laid another picture beside it. "And this one. The Stark house is quite pretty, about the right size, and it's nicely maintained. It has new air and heat, but the price reflects that, I'm afraid. The Morris house doesn't." She added a picture of a dilapidated Victorian to the spread. "I imagine you'd want to put in central air, since you're not used to our, uh, hot summers."

Lauren didn't react as Mosey expected to the run-down state of the Morris house. She eyed it with a faint air of curiosity and asked, "How much does a house like that cost?"

"The Morris house? One hundred thirty thousand, but that's the asking price. We can make a lower offer if you want."

Lauren's eyebrows rose above her tortoise shell frames. "Actually, that doesn't sound bad to me. Not at all."

"Of course, it doesn't. You're accustomed to the Philadelphia market. Everything in Hembree's going to sound like a bargain. But you need to be careful. Should you decide to sell, you wouldn't get more than what you paid, plus, hopefully, what you spent on the remodel."

She continued showing Lauren snapshots of properties in her price range until she'd covered the entire desk in pictures of old houses. "What appeals to you?"

"Let's start with these." She picked up three. "This is my favorite—" She held up the Eldridge house. "—

but these two are nice."

Saffron peeked in, then entered with mugs and a carafe of coffee on a tray. "Where you want this?"

Mosey cleared a spot on the edge of the desk. "Here, I'll take it."

"You need anything else?"

"This is good, thanks." Mosey nodded at Saffron as she left, then, pointing to the photograph of the Eldridge house, said to Lauren, "How'd you happen to see that one? Not to pry, but—"

"I was checking out historic homes in the area." Pausing, Lauren looked down at her business skirt, ran her hand over it as if to smooth out wrinkles—of which there were none. "Someone must have mentioned it when I was here for the interview."

"Really." Mosey filled the mugs, served Lauren and herself, and settled back in her chair.

"I met a man one night at the Tavernette bar," she said. "We were making small talk, and he asked me if I'd had a chance to look at real estate in Hembree. I'd mentioned I was hoping to move here in late fall. I said I hadn't had a chance, and he started telling me about the Historic District, though he clearly preferred some other part of town, on the outskirts, he said."

"Which is where the Eldridge house is."

She nodded. "So, I took a look—"

"On the Hembree website?"

She nodded again.

"Did he mention this house specifically?" Mosey asked.

"I don't think so, but he did say he had an eye on a house in Cottonwood Acres."

"Yeah, that's in the same area." Mosey propped her

15

elbow on the desk. "I was curious…well, the Eldridge house hasn't listed yet, and it's unusual to get a request on an unlisted property unless, of course, the family's involved."

Mosey, stop snooping, child. You want to blow this deal to smithereens?

Her deceased father's intervention was timely, given that Mosey, whose curiosity often overruled her sense of propriety, was on the verge of saying, "I don't guess you remember the fellow's name, do you?" Instead, she tapped her knuckles lightly on the desk. "Tell you what. Before we drive over there, let me give John Earle a call. It was supposed to list last week. Not sure what the hold-up is." She stood and reached into her tote for her cell. "Why don't we start with the Morris house. It's just around the corner. Then let's check out the Stark house. It's about a mile out of town. Maybe we'll have heard from John Earle by then."

"Sounds good," Lauren said as she set down her mug and picked up her coat.

On their way past reception, they said goodbye to Saffron. Then the two of them headed out to see houses.

Chapter Three

Mosey and Lauren took off for the Morris house, which was a short distance from Shepherd Realty. "This street has some of the prettiest and oldest houses," Mosey said as she rounded the corner onto McAllister. "That's a former dean's house over there." She nodded toward the Baker property. "His daughter lives there now, but she'll be moving soon, I imagine. Next door is the Waites' old place and across the street—see that Queen Anne? That's the Raines house."

"Gorgeous homes, all of them," Lauren said. "Beautiful trees and gardens."

"Yeah, this is the Historic District, very old, very nice. The Morris house is farther down, at the dead end…not quite as kept up."

As they approached the last house on McAllister, Mosey geared herself up for putting a good spin on a property that in recent years had seriously declined. "This is the Morris house, built around 1900. It's not as old as some, but it's a charming place, pretty much fits your specs."

"This is a great house," Lauren said. "The exterior looks, well, not so bad."

"You're generous." Mosey downshifted and slowly

bumped her way into the drive. "I'm afraid some of my clients would back away in horror." She got out and retrieved the key from the drop box attached to the gate.

Though Boo Radley could have easily been hiding behind the elaborately worked trim at the porch entrance—a sort of arch, big and curvy, with spandrels and brackets all around, like a monstrous spider web—Lauren just stepped up on the deteriorating planks and said, "This is a Stick Victorian, isn't it?"

"Yes, most of the houses in this part of town are either Sticks or Queen Annes, with some Arts and Crafts on the newer streets. When I was a kid, I called this the half-house."

"Why's that?" Lauren cast her eyes from post to post on the wide front porch.

"It's as if the builder started out with a cross floor plan and ran out of money. It's similar to my parents' house—my house now. Believe me, this place has seen better days. But give it a good power washing and a fresh coat of paint, and it'd look really nice. Let's go inside, if you don't mind a little dust." Mosey slipped her hand in her pocket for a cautionary handkerchief, then unlocked the door. "Watch your step."

Lauren entered a step or two ahead of her and, after a quick look around, ran her fingers over the papered wall. "I don't mind the pattern. It's not as fussy as some I've seen, but wallpaper's out, isn't it?"

"It is," Mosey said with a cough. "But in these old homes, it can be the best option, unless you want to rip out the plaster and put in sheetrock."

"The woodwork's in good shape," Lauren said, scrutinizing one of four tall mahogany doors that led from the foyer into the adjacent rooms.

"Yeah, these doors were all wood-grained," Mosey said. "It took a talented craftsman to do that."

"That's not the natural grain?"

"Nope, all painted on."

They took a quick look at the parlor and the master bedroom, both of which were off the foyer, before entering the hall that ran along the right side of the house. "If the builder had completed the initial floor plan," Mosey said, "I bet there'd be a dining room right there and maybe a half-bath off the dining room. You could finish out the cross, or you could leave it like it is and use the kitchen as a dining space."

At the end of the hall, Mosey pushed back the swinging door to the kitchen, and as they crossed the room, the floor, which was covered in the original linoleum, made the same squeaking noise her floors made before the remodel. "As you can see, they've put a partition between the work area and the breakfast nook. You could move that old hot water heater if you want." She crossed over to the pantry and opened the door. "Plenty of room in here." She closed the door and walked back to the center of the room.

Lauren, staring down at the floor, didn't seem to be paying much attention.

"Our floors—" Mosey glanced down. "—weren't much better. We pulled up the linoleum and found loblolly pine. Finished up beautifully. I imagine you'd find that here."

"Hey, a wood floor would be beautiful—" Lauren looked up. "—but how much would that cost?"

"About two thousand."

"Not bad." Lauren scanned the layout of the kitchen. She opened a couple of cabinets, then followed Mosey back down the hall.

"What do you think so far?" Mosey asked.

"I love the tall ceilings, the trim, the floor-to ceiling windows. This is an amazing place."

"Yeah, it is, if a little scrubbing and painting don't put you off."

"I think it's okay. I mean, I wouldn't have to do anything major right away."

"It has a lot of charm."

"There's no bath on this floor?"

"Afraid not. But you could easily add a half-bath in the master bedroom. The room's plenty big, twenty by twenty."

By now they had rambled their way from the kitchen back to the foyer, and Lauren, peering up into the dark void of the second story, said, "I'd like to see the upstairs."

"Sure." Mosey flipped the light switch, illuminating the crystal chandelier, and led the way up the stairs.

"What's up here?" Lauren asked.

"Three bedrooms and a bath, with the original footed tub. No shower, though."

"The stairs seem sturdy."

"Oh, yeah. These houses are often better built than the new ones."

They reached the landing, and Lauren pushed open the door on the left. "Oh, my."

"What?"

"Check this out. They've left the furniture and drapes."

"Hmm, they didn't mention anything about that."

"Who's 'they'?" Lauren asked.

"The Morris heirs, the two daughters. Their brother

died years ago. Would you want the furniture?"

"I'd have to think about it, but maybe. I hardly have any of my own."

Mosey walked to the closest window and pushed back the drapes, made of a dark fig-colored fabric. Light poured into the room.

"Look at the poster bed," Lauren said. "Wow, this is a nice one." She sat and bounced a couple of times. "Mattress and bed springs seem to be in good shape."

"I love this old dresser," Mosey said. "I believe it's walnut—yep, I think so. And look at that." She gestured toward a marble-top nightstand by the bed. "Pieces like this are hard to come by."

As they were finishing their tour of the second story, Mosey's phone rang. "Hold on a second. It's John Earle." She leaned against the banister at the top of the stairs. "What's up?"

"You with Lauren now?"

"Yeah, we're at the Morris place, just leaving. But speaking of which, there's furniture in one of the upstairs bedrooms. You know anything about that?"

"Hmm. Nobody mentioned it to me. Why, does Lauren want it?"

"She might, if she decides to take the house."

"Look," John Earle said, changing the subject, "I wanted to get back with you about the Eldridge house. We still don't have the property disclosure and listing agreement forms, but the owner says go ahead and show the house."

"Okay, great. I'll let you know after she sees it if she's interested. Like I said, we're just now leaving the Morris house."

"Don't fall through the cracks."

"Haven't seen any cracks. Plenty of dust and spider webs. By the way, where'd you put the key to the Eldridge house?"

"In the flowerpot next to the front door."

"Okay, thanks. Appreciate the update." She dropped the phone in her purse and looked at Lauren, who was waiting in the foyer below. "Did you follow that?"

"Not really."

"I can show you the Eldridge house. The owner says it's okay."

"Oh, good. Could we go there now?"

Mosey glanced at her watch. "It's a short drive out of town, but I think we have plenty of time. When do you need to be back?"

"Robert mentioned getting together for lunch."

"Okay, that gives us about an hour."

They headed back down McAllister and took Little Smith toward Cottonwood Acres, which had grown up higgledy-piggledy in a farming area close to the Mississippi River. As they arrived at the Eldridge house, Mosey spotted a car in the garage. "That's strange. The house has been empty since the owners moved to the Magnolia. That's the assisted living back down the road."

"Maybe they don't need a car. Are they still active?"

"Not so much." She parked and walked up the sidewalk, stopping to retrieve the key from a large urn-shaped planter near the entrance. She unlocked the door and held it back. "Before you go in, notice the fantail light transom above the door."

"Yeah, I remember it from the picture. Very pretty."

"I love the façade and the porch," Mosey said. "The wood siding is in good shape. That's a fine paint job, and the color's nice—if you like red...well, it's a dark red. Not bad."

"How old *is* this house?"

"Very. One of the oldest around here. I'd guess around 1850. When we get the specs, I imagine it will say," she said, walking in. "It's about the same square-footage as the last house, even though it's only one story. Both are around 2,000 square feet, and both have three bedrooms. But this one has the advantage of having a bath and a half."

"Not as much of a fixer-upper," Lauren said.

"The price is likely to be higher, though," she said with a half-smile. "Of course, we don't know that yet."

Lauren closed the door behind them. "I would expect to pay more for this one."

"The floor plan is rectangular," Mosey said, "and it's my understanding that if you were to take up the carpet, you'd find heart of pine flooring throughout."

"Any way we could check?"

"The specs will say." She crossed the foyer and glanced down the long hall. "You've got a central foyer in this one. The living room and dining room are on the left, the bedrooms on the right, and the kitchen at the back. There's a bath off the hall, conveniently located between the bedrooms and across from the living room."

Lauren peeked in. "Pretty. Looks like the fixtures have been updated."

"You might put in a shower over the tub. Wouldn't cost much."

"Maybe...after I get settled." She followed Mosey into the living room.

"There're beautiful plantation shutters in here. Let me open some of these." She opened a shutter on the far side of the room—less for Lauren's benefit than her own. She wanted to get a closer look at the garage. As she did, deep indentations between the frame and the sill caught her attention—jimmy marks, as if someone had tried to open the window with a crowbar. She quickly closed the shutters. "Huh. Not sure whose car that is in the garage. Maybe John Earle will know." She turned to Lauren. "Let's see the rest of the house."

"This carpeting isn't bad," Lauren said. "I might want to keep it."

"It's soft on the feet. I'll give it that." Mosey led the way from the living room into an ample dining area. "This is a good-sized space. Plenty big enough for a table and eight chairs—if you like to entertain," she added. "But you could just as well turn it into a home office."

"And it opens into the kitchen. I like that," Lauren said as she entered the sizeable country kitchen.

"Yeah, and you've got two entrances," Mosey said, "one from the dining room and the other from the hall."

"They haven't updated here." Lauren eyed the old model range, then opened the oven door.

"No, and this would be your only real expense. If you're interested, we could get some rough estimates. There's a kitchen design store off the Square."

They checked the appliances and cabinets, then took the back steps down to the patio. Mosey paused to admire the dominant feature of the fenced-in yard—a live oak surrounded by pave stones. "You'll appreciate that big tree, if you decide on this place. It'll keep the back of the house cool, and you won't have to worry about the sun blinding you when you're cooking supper."

"I'd love a live oak," Lauren said. "Very Southern."

Though the tall, triangular-shaped specimen wasn't a bona fide Southern live oak, it was a live oak all the same and common to the Delta region. At that point Mosey was wishing for a little more "Southern" and a little less "gothic," because, as soon as she had spotted the jimmy marks on the inside of the window, the beautiful old home had acquired an air of eeriness. How did those marks get there? Had the window been stuck, and somebody had tried to pry it open with a crowbar? She herself had dented some sills in her own house, jimmying windows that had been painted shut. But surely someone, in readying the house to go on the market, would have sanded and repainted the sill.

Though anxious to bring the scrutiny of the property to a close, Mosey's preoccupation with the car prodded her to stay. "I'm still curious about whose car that is." She opened the garden gate and, passing into the garage, stared through the windshield. "Hmm. I doubt the Eldridges—" She stopped and, gasping, clasped her hands over her mouth.

Lauren, a few steps behind, having stopped to admire the ferns along the fence, called out as she entered the garage, "Mosey, what is it?"

"Stop, Lauren," she said, throwing up her hands. "Stop right there. Don't look."

"Don't look at what?"

"Th-th-there's a man..." Mosey edged toward Lauren. "He's not moving," she said, eyes winced shut. "I'm pretty sure he's dead."

Chapter Four

November 2, 1:00 p.m.
The Eldridge House—otherwise Sunny Banks

Lauren waited in the truck while Mosey paced along the drive, sputtering out answers to the 911 dispatcher's questions. She clicked off and gave Lauren a thumbs up, then tapped in Robert's number but got his voice mail. "Robert, call me soon as you hear this. I need someone, preferably you or Hugh, to pick up Lauren. We've got an emergency at the Eldridge house, 313 Little Smith. I'll explain later." She called Hugh next and, also getting his voice mail, left a similar message.

She went back to the garage and jotted down the plate number of the car. It was an Arkansas tag. She didn't recognize the make right off but, once she had located the logo and model number, saw that it was a Tyche-XL500. She approached the driver's window and peered in at the victim. His head, neck, and shoulders were covered in blood.

"Mosey."

She turned as Sergeant Springer entered the garage.

"What we got here?" he said.

"I'm pretty sure he's dead. It's locked. I tried the door." Indeed, she'd tried all the doors and even the trunk but had found no way in.

"So, you touched the door, did you?"

"Sorry, I wasn't sure he was dead. I thought—"

"Well, I might have done the same myself. He could have been alive."

She backed away voluntarily, knowing at any moment he would tell her to leave the crime scene.

"If you wouldn't mind waiting over there." Springer gestured toward her truck. "Who's that with you, by the way?"

"A client," she said, "Lauren Wilson. I was showing her the house."

"I imagine the chief will have some questions, but in the meantime—" He glanced over at her. "—I need to secure the scene."

"Of course. I'll get out of your way." As she headed to the truck, she crossed paths with Reagan, who was hurrying toward the garage, an orange cone in each hand.

Springer yelled to Reagan, "We're gonna need the lock-out tool and a stretcher."

She continued on to the truck, and Reagan, heading back to the SUV, walked around her.

"I thought Lieutenant Olivera was coming," Mosey said to Reagan.

The middle-aged officer—who wore a duty rig around his waist as heavy as he was—tipped his peaked hat as he passed. "Yes, ma'am, he's comin'. But don't you worry. Me and Springer can take care of it till he gets here."

Mosey wasn't so confident that they could, but she went on to the truck and climbed in.

Lauren shook her head. "I never imagined the morning would turn out like this."

"Yeah, I know what you mean. He's dead—the man in the car—I'm pretty sure." She drummed her fingers against the steering wheel. "Gosh, I wish Lieutenant Olivera would get here."

Slipping down in her seat, Mosey looked out at the tree-line across the road. A scrubby assembly of box elders, silver maples, and river birches—the kind of trees that usually grew on vacant lots—stretched along the ditch bank that separated the empty field from Little Smith. The closest house was a good five hundred yards away. Most anything could have happened at the Eldridge house, especially under the cover of night, and no one would have been the wiser.

The sound of tires on gravel rose behind her, and she checked the rearview mirror. The coroner's vehicle had pulled up and stopped. "That's Eads McGinnis." She rolled down the window and called out as she motioned to Eads, "They're in the garage. Go around that way."

Eads approached the car window. "You guys find the body?"

"Yeah." Mosey exhaled deeply. "I was showing the house to Lauren here—this is Lauren Wilson."

Eads nodded, then, turned back to Mosey. "You recognize the victim?"

She shook her head. "I couldn't see his face."

Eads, equipment in hand, continued on and, stopping a short distance from the garage, slipped into protective gear.

"I'm so sorry," Mosey said to Lauren. "This is *not* the introduction to Hembree I would have wanted for you."

Of course, it's not the introduction you'd have wanted. But I don't know, girl. How many stigmatized houses does this make?

She responded to her fussy, omnipresent father with

28

an eyeroll and, turning to Lauren, said, "I've called Robert and Hugh and left messages for somebody to pick you up."

Lauren didn't answer, just sat quietly, hands folded in her lap, not fidgeting, as Mosey tended to do when she was nervous.

"Can I get you anything?" Mosey asked.

"Another cup of coffee would be nice." She eyed the thermos in Mosey's tote.

Mosey smiled. "I happen to have a thermos with me." She reached into her tote for the thermos and filled the lid. "Drink some of this. It'll warm you right up."

The sound of tires on gravel came again. It was Olivera. He pulled into the drive and, getting out, frowned briefly at Mosey's truck before striding toward the garage.

Her phone hummed. "Robert…glad it's you."

"What's going on?"

"Lauren and I are at Sunny Banks. You know the place?"

"Yeah."

"Okay…I can't leave just yet. There's a body in the garage, but—"

"A body? What do you mean *a body*?"

"What I said. The police and Eads are here. Olivera is gonna have questions, but I don't want Lauren to be stuck in the middle of this."

"I'll be there, soon as I can get away."

Robert arrived just as Eads, with Springer and Reagan's help, was loading the body into the back of the van.

Olivera came out of the garage, said something to Eads, then approached Mosey's truck.

"Lieutenant—" Mosey rolled down the window. "—you don't need Lauren to stay, do you? She didn't see anything, and Robert's here to take her back to town." She gestured toward Robert's car.

"I suppose you have a key to the house?" Olivera said.

"I do, but it's still open."

"Let's go in. I have a few questions."

"Lauren, too?"

He nodded. "Lauren, too."

The three of them entered the house, and Olivera positioned himself in front of the fireplace before turning his attention to her and Lauren. "Why don't you have a seat over there." He gestured toward the window seat to the left of the fireplace. "Okay," he began, "just a few questions now—" He pulled out a note pad and pencil. "—but I want to see both of you later at the station."

He jotted down the preliminaries, then looked up, his soft brown eyes now focused on Mosey. "Tell me why you were here and how you happened to discover the body."

"I was showing Lauren the house. She's my first prospective buyer for the property."

"Has your agency listed the house?"

"Not yet," she said, then hurriedly added, "but John Earle got permission for me to show it."

"But you haven't listed it."

"No, but the paperwork should be complete soon." She stressed "soon." He easily put her on the defensive, as she did him.

"When did you arrive?" he continued.

"Around twelve fifteen. About then, wasn't it?" She turned to Lauren, who agreed with a dip of her chin.

"And what did you do exactly?"

"What did I do? Well," she stammered, "I showed Lauren the inside of the house, right, Lauren?"

"That's right."

"Then we walked out to the back." She motioned. "Actually, come to think of it, I noticed some strange marks on the windowsill over there." She nodded toward the window in question. "I opened the shutters to let in some light and saw a car in the garage—more accurately, I had noticed it when we first drove up. So, I went to the window to take a look. Seemed strange, a car here—the house has been empty a good while." She stopped and swallowed hard. "And then I spotted the jimmy marks."

"Jimmy marks."

"Yeah, jimmy marks."

"Right." He jotted something down and continued, "Then you went outside?"

"No, I finished showing Lauren the house, and we left by the back."

"And you went into the garage?"

"Yes, after a quick walk around the yard. I hadn't been here before."

"And what did you see?"

"A man slumped over the steering wheel."

"Did you try to open the door?"

"Yes, I thought he might be alive. But it was locked. Then I went around to the passenger side. It was locked, too."

"Dr. Wilson—" He turned to a fresh page. "—did you see the body?"

"No, Mosey told me to get in the truck. It was obvious something, well, I don't know—"

"It was clear something had happened, and she

didn't want you to see?"

"Yes, that's right. I returned to the truck and got in."

He paused, flipping back through his notes. "Anything else?"

"No, that's about it," Lauren said.

"You're from out of town, right?"

"I am."

"Stick around if you can till we clear up a few things."

"I was planning to stay a couple of days."

"Good. And please drop by the station…both of you." He looked at Lauren, then Mosey. "We'll need a written statement and a signature."

"Sure, Lieutenant," Lauren said. "No problem."

Chapter Five

November 2, 2:00 p.m.
Morgue, Delta Infirmary

"Dr. McGinnis—" Olivera smiled. "What have we got?" He removed his hat, tossed it toward the rack in the corner, and approached the gurney. In the workplace, he was still calling her by her surname despite his growing personal interest in the petite brunette.

"White male, late thirties." She uncovered the body and offered him a handkerchief scented in something minty. "No serious injuries, other than a laceration on the back of the head." She tilted the victim's head, exposing the wound. "Slightly below the HBL, looks like."

He drew closer. "The cause of death, I suppose." He examined the gash, then stepped back.

"Probably. Let's say it *could* have been." Her eyes fell on the wound. "The skull is cracked through."

"Why the doubt, then?" To him, it seemed pretty cut and dried.

"I've still got the blood work to do, and I've got to examine the contents of the stomach, but if I don't find anything else, well, more compelling—"

"More compelling?" he cut in, perplexed.

Her eyes, circled by horn rims, turned up to him. "There's a good bit of blood on the clothing and the car seat. We're safe in assuming he fell or was bludgeoned

33

before he was put in the car."

"I didn't see any blood stains outside the car, did you?"

"No, no visible foot prints, either. But we'll have to recheck all that."

"Did you get a time of death?"

"The body was in full rigor. Ball park, a good twelve hours, maybe more, prior to discovery."

"So," he said, "whatever it was must have happened last night. What else you got?"

"I don't see any defensive wounds on the hands." She picked up the victim's right hand and turned it over. "No cuts or scratches, but he might have attacked his assailant some other way. We can gather that there wasn't a serious altercation, given the lack of abrasions." She lifted the sheet, exposing the victim's feet. "Slight bruising at the ankles."

"He was dragged?"

"I'd say so." She covered the lower half, then uncovered the top half down to the abdomen. "And there's this."

"Bruising to the chest."

"Classical resuscitation pattern," she said.

"So, somebody tried to resuscitate the victim?"

"I would conclude that, provisionally."

"But, of course, we can't say who," he said. "Must have been the assailant, if there *was* an assailant. Or someone else, I suppose, might have come along—" He paused. "No, that wouldn't make sense. If someone had come along, surely they would have reported the accident."

"That's it so far."

"Okay, Dr. McGinnis, what are you thinking?"

She tossed her gloves in the trash and dropped her readers in the pocket of her lab coat. "I'm not sure we even have a crime, Lieutenant, well, not a homicide."

He took a step back. "Why's that?"

"No defensive wounds, nothing to suggest a struggle, not even a ripped seam. Plus—" She gestured toward the victim's head. "—the head wound—it's not just a skin lesion. It's a fracture, which is what you would expect from a hard fall. He could have hit his head against a table or a mantel piece or any blunt object—the edge of a step, a cabinet, a bookcase, something not as sharp-edged as a knife, more round-edged, like a bathtub or lavatory."

"How do you know somebody didn't whack him over the head with a tire iron?"

"It's possible, but the position of the wound, below the hat brim line, is more likely the result of a fall."

"So, then, Doctor, how do we clear this up?" He paced around the gurney, eyes shifting between the body and the coroner.

"Give me a couple of hours to perform an autopsy," she said, "run some tests. And I need the crime scene evidence. By the way, we're calling the car the death scene, not the primary crime scene, right?"

He nodded.

"Which means," she continued, "we need to establish where the incident occurred."

He stopped, looking again at the bruising on the chest and the head wound. "I'll check the house again."

"Yes, and the yard."

"I suppose he might have fallen against a concrete bench," he said, "or one of those—what do you call them?"

"Garden ornaments?" she suggested.

"Yeah." He turned toward the door, as if to leave, then turned back. "Come to think of it, what about his clothes? Any mud, grass?"

"Nothing noticeable, but I'll have to recheck it."

"We've towed the car to the station," he said. "Springer will bag anything suspicious."

"Sounds good."

During the last minute of conversation, Olivera had retrieved his hat, which he now stood nervously spinning. He put it on his head and checked his watch. "It's 2:20. I'll send Springer over...soon as he's finished. And I'll be back. Three, four o'clock?"

"Fine, but call first."

"Why?" he asked.

"In case I hit a snag. I wouldn't want to waste your time." She batted her eyes.

He smiled. "Sure thing, Doc."

Chapter Six

Police Garage, Hembree
November 2, 2:45 p.m.

"You gotta wonder, Chief—" Springer scratched his head. "—why the assailant put the victim in the driver's seat when it would have been easier to put him in the trunk." He walked around to the trunk and popped it open. "There's plenty of room back here." With gloved hands, he lifted the spare tire and laid it on the evidence table. "All he had to do is get rid of this here tire and this other stuff." He pulled out a jack and bag of tools and laid them on the table next to the tire.

"I don't know, Springer." Olivera approached the table. "Dr. McGinnis says we don't even know if we're talking murder here."

"You gotta be kidding me," he said, palpable the annoyance in his voice.

"I just came from the morgue. She hasn't finished her investigation, barely started, actually, but she says there's no clear evidence of foul play."

Springer pursed his lips and looked askance at Olivera. "I don't see why she'd say that."

"That head gash is below the hat brim line, which suggests a fall. An intentional blow is likely to hit higher." He tapped the back of Springer's head with the side of his hand. "Know what I mean?"

"Right, but what about the death scene? He didn't crack open his skull, get in the car, and sit there waiting to bleed out."

"Nope, unlikely he did that—" Olivera raised his brow. "—unless somebody came along behind him and cleaned up the mess."

"Somebody *put* him in that car, Chief." Springer shook his head hard. "You can count on it."

"I imagine so, but why in the driver's seat, as you said before? Why didn't he put him in the trunk?" Olivera leaned against the table, facing Springer. "Think about it. If you offed a guy, why would you put him in the driver's seat when it'd be easier to put him in the trunk or the passenger's seat? There wouldn't be a steering wheel to get in the way. Why put him in a car at all—" He threw up his hands. "—then go off and leave the car in the garage? Why not drive to the river, dump the body—?" Olivera stopped, allowing his mind to wander in a slightly different direction. "Hey, we're forgetting something."

"What, Chief?"

"The house, Sunny Banks they call it. So, there must be a body of water around there somewhere, a pond, a small creek, maybe."

"Yeah, that's right."

"You know of any water around there, Springer?"

"Why, the river's hardly any distance at all."

"What about back in the woods?"

Springer didn't answer, just rubbed his chin and stared into thin air.

"When do you expect to be finished here?"

"A half-hour, hour at most." Springer put on a pair of goggles and picked up a UV lamp. "I've got to go over the interior. I thought I'd start with the UV."

"Soon as you finish, take whatever you find over to the morgue. Then, I want you and Reagan to go back to the property, take enough cones to cordon off the yard. Look all around the back. See if you can find something, a ditch, creek, and keep an eye out for blood stains, any little speck you see."

"Will do."

"And another thing. Ms. Frye said she noticed some jimmy marks on one of the living room windows. See if you can pick up any prints. And check to see if we've got Ms. Frye's prints on file. I bet we do. When she and Lauren Wilson come in, get Wilson's, too."

"Sure, Chief."

"By the way, what'd you get on the license?"

"The car's registered to the owner of the house," Springer said, "Old Man Eldridge."

"Snazzy car for an old man."

"You know these old rich dudes, how they are. Riding around in snazzy convertibles, picking up women."

Olivera laughed. "So that's what you're looking forward to in old age?"

"Not me, Chief."

"You know I was just thinking. It's sort of a slap in the face to Eldridge to dump a corpse in this fancy car of his." He peeked in at the gray leather interior.

"I doubt he'll be using it any time soon," Springer said. "He's over at the Magnolia, or so I hear."

"Magnolia Nursing Home?"

"Yeah, he and his wife both. My niece works for 'em, gets 'em whatever they need, takes 'em places."

"No family around to do that sort of thing?" Olivera

asked.

"They've got family, but I guess they're used to hiring people to do for 'em."

"I expect so. Come to think of it, I ought to contact Ms. Frye, see what she can tell me about the sellers." Olivera headed out the garage door. "See you later this afternoon."

Chapter Seven

November 2, 3:00 p.m.
Shepherd Realty

Mosey and Lauren caught a quick bite with Robert at the Tavernette, then squeezed in a visit to the Stark house, which, disappointingly, had neither the charm of the Morris house nor the polish of the Eldridge house. After dropping Lauren at the Social Sciences Building, Mosey returned to Shepherd Realty.

She was pacing around the office, pulling her thoughts together, when the phone rang. "Mosey Frye here."

"Ms. Frye?"

"That you, Lieutenant?"

"Yes, I have some questions about the Eldridge property. I'm on my way out and thought I'd stop by your office, if you don't mind."

"Sure, Lieutenant. I'll be around for a while." She glanced at the digital clock on the wall. "I've got about an hour. You coming now?"

"I'll be there in five, ten minutes."

She put the receiver back on the hook and walked down the hall to the main office. "That was Lieutenant Olivera," she said to Saffron. "He's dropping by. If I get any calls while he's here, will you hold them, please, ma'am?"

Saffron got up from her desk. "I guess the lieutenant will want a cup of coffee, you reckon?"

"Have you got any of those pecan tarts left?"

"I do, but I was thinking about taking them to Uncle T. Patrick."

At the mention of Saffron's great-great uncle, Mosey remembered that both he and the Eldridges were at the Magnolia Nursing Home. "I guess you heard the Eldridges are at the Magnolia, too." She followed Saffron into the coffee niche.

"Is that right?" Saffron poured the leftover coffee down the drain and rinsed out the pot.

"Wonder if anybody's told them about Sunny Banks." Mosey perched on a stool next to the counter.

"I kind of doubt it," Saffron said with a scrunch of her nose. "People don't like to upset old folks, not if they can help it."

"It's *their* house. They'd better tell them before they read about it in the paper." Mosey stood and paced away, stopping under the arch that led to the hall. "When I left, they were cordoning off the garage, but I imagine the whole property will be off limits, wouldn't you think?"

"I don't know," Saffron said. "If the body was in the car, you have to wonder if maybe he wasn't killed in the house."

"Uh-huh, that's just what I was thinking." Mosey walked back into the niche. "Unlikely he was killed outside where anybody passing down Little Smith could see." She scratched her head. "You know, it's funny. When we were over there this morning, I didn't see any sign of a disturbance. Wait a minute…I *did* see something, jimmy marks on one of the windowsills. I opened the shutters on the far side of the living room, thinking I'd take a look at the car again. I'd noticed it when we drove up, but then I saw the dents in the sill and closed the shutters right quick before Lauren could see."

"Huh. Any sign of anything in the yard?" Saffron set a fresh pot of water on to boil.

"Nothing, not a thing."

"You think he could have been killed somewhere else, then hauled over there?"

Mosey shrugged. "Maybe. You'd think, if he was killed there, there'd be some sign of a scuffle. I didn't see anything really, inside or out. I guess they'll be going over every inch of the place."

"Wonder what Olivera wants," Saffron said.

"Whatever he can prod out of me."

The door opened, and Mosey wheeled around. Olivera had entered reception, hat in hand.

"Lieutenant," Mosey said. "Didn't hear you drive up."

"I walked over."

"Can we offer you some coffee? Saffron was just making a pot."

"Yes, thank you. I'd appreciate that." He nodded to Saffron.

"Let's go into my office," Mosey said.

He followed her in.

"Have a seat."

Olivera sat in the chair across from the desk. "As I'm sure you've surmised, we've opened an investigation into the death of the victim."

Mosey nodded and sat in her swivel chair.

"So," he began, "what sort of arrangement do you have with the seller?"

"I explained that this morning. We *will be* the lister

43

when the paper work is complete."

"But you had permission to show the property to Lauren Wilson *only*, right?"

"That's right," she said with a half-frown. She picked up the picture of the Eldridge house, stacked it on top of the pictures of the Morris and Stark houses, and slipped them into a folder.

"Let's see if I've got this right." He pulled out his tablet. "The property known as Sunny Banks is owned by Martin and Dorothy Eldridge, currently residents of the Magnolia Nursing Home. I'm guessing someone other than the elderly couple spoke with Shepherd Realty about listing the property."

"John Earle spoke with somebody, but he didn't say who. One of the Eldridges, but I'm not sure which one."

"Can you find out for me? I'd like to speak to them."

"Certainly, I'll call John Earle, or, come to think of it, Saffron might know." She got up from her chair. "Hold on a second." She stepped into the hall. "Saffron, you know who's managing Sunny Banks for the Eldridges?"

"I can check the file."

"Yes, please do."

Saffron, who had filled a tray with cups, sugar, cream, and a squat carafe of coffee, followed Mosey back to her office. "Here's your coffee." She set the tray on the desk.

"Thank you, ma'am." Olivera waited for Saffron to pour, then sprinkled in a packet of sugar.

"Lieutenant," Saffron said with a grin, "I see you've picked up some of our local expressions."

He smiled. "Yes, ma'am, I suppose I have."

"People in California don't say 'ma'am,' do they?"

"I reckon not." He laughed.

Saffron left, and Mosey returned to her seat. "If you don't mind my asking, Lieutenant, where *do* we, I mean Lauren and I, stand as far as Sunny Banks is concerned?"

"It's off limits till we've had a chance to pick up what evidence we can." He paused to stir his coffee. "Those jimmy marks, by the way... You remember touching the window?"

"The shutters, yes, but the window—" She slowly shook her head. "—I don't think so."

"Do we have your prints on file?"

"I'm sure you do." She lowered her brow.

Saffron entered the room again. "Here you go, Lieutenant." She handed him a page from her yellow note pad. "That's the name and contact information. It's Jack Eldridge, the old couple's son."

"Thank you." He smiled and nodded to Saffron as she headed out, then set his cup down and tucked the note into his tablet. Turning to Mosey, he said, "So, you haven't been in touch with Jack Eldridge—is that right?"

"No, I haven't, but I imagine I will, when the forms come in."

"Forms?"

"The listing form and the property disclosure form."

"I see, but you must have *some* information on the property. You have a potential buyer, do you not?"

"Lauren seems particularly interested, but she's looking at some other places, too. We were at the old Morris house before Sunny Banks, and then—"

"She didn't mention," he cut in, "*why* she was 'particularly interested' in the Eldridge house, did she?"

"Well, to tell you the truth, we hadn't been there fifteen minutes when that body showed up, but I know she wants an old house, a fixer-upper, and she's in a hurry to find something. She has to get moved in before spring semester. You know she's the new hire in Psychology at Blanchard." She paused. Should she tell him about the conversation between Lauren and the guy she'd met at the Tavernette? It seemed like a flimsy lead. Probably better not to mention it.

Olivera went on jotting in his tablet, then stopped and looked up. "Do you happen to know why the property is called Sunny Banks?"

"Huh, hadn't really thought about it, but I guess at one time there must have been a pond or creek somewhere around there. I haven't examined the property or researched it, but as soon as we list it—"

"So, Ms. Frye," he interrupted—impatient man that he was—, "you haven't seen a creek or a pond on or near the property?"

"There're ponds and lakes and creeks all over the place—"

"Right."

"—and with the river changing course and flooding ever now and again, there might have been a creek or pond on the land behind the house. Could have disappeared when the water level dropped."

"Just how old is the house, by the way?" he asked.

"Well, the architectural style was popular in the mid-nineteenth century, but the oldest building in Hembree, far as I know, is the Tavernette, and it was built—at least re-built—after the Civil War. I'd guess Sunny Banks dates from about then."

"Has it been in Eldridge hands very long?"

"It belonged to the Eldridges going back as far as my grandfather's time. My father was in school with the

Eldridge kids."

Olivera took a sip of coffee, then dropped his tablet and pencil into his coat pocket. "Thank you for the information—and the coffee. I'll be back in touch as soon as I get the coroner's report and we know what we're dealing with." He took another sip and stood.

"Certainly, Lieutenant."

"I'd like to speak with you again…and with Dr. Wilson."

"No problem," she said. "I'll see you out."

"I know the way."

After he'd left, Mosey wandered back toward reception. "That's funny."

"What?"

"Olivera." She leaned against Saffron's desk. "He came here for a few little pieces of information about the house, stuff I could have just as easily given him over the phone."

"Yeah." She looked up at Mosey. "Maybe he was on a fishing expedition."

"He probably thinks I know more than I do." Mosey drifted back toward her office, rubbing her chin. "Look at that," she said as she passed through the door. "He didn't even drink his coffee, well, not much of it." She set the cup on the tray and carried it back to the coffee niche. "Sometimes that man is just one big waste of time. I don't know what Eads sees in him."

Saffron chuckled.

"What are you laughing at?"

"Nothing, nothing at all."

Chapter Eight

November 2, late afternoon
The Tavernette, Hembree

Lauren sat quietly across from Mosey. She took a sip of beer, then stared into the foam.

Mosey wasn't feeling especially buoyant herself. She preferred to be anywhere else: gabbing with Nadia at the shop, hashing over the events of the morning with Robert, or chewing the fat with Saffron. In view of the goings-on at the Eldridge property, she and Saffron certainly had some fat to chew. "So, Lauren," she said, "have you come to any conclusion about the houses?"

"I liked Sunny Banks best, but now..."

"I know." Mosey shook her head. "My fault, probably."

"Your fault?" Lauren wrinkled her forehead.

"I've been doing this—selling houses—for a little over a year. Sometimes I think I'm a magnet for stigmatized properties."

"Stigmatized," Lauren repeated.

"Yeah, you know, houses where a bad something-or-other has been committed, like a murder, suicide, whatever. Take my first sale, Waite House, scene of a murder six months before it went on the market. We passed it on the way to the Morris house. Big Victorian, long flight of steps, veranda, pretty old house across from the Queen Anne."

The Queen Anne, where the blooming—

Mosey cut off her daddy's intrusion with an icy stare, then went on, "I don't know what to advise. You could wait, see if the police can clear this up. Olivera's sort of new, came from California. He's pretty good at his job."

"Not sure I have the luxury of waiting."

"Or—" Mosey sipped her beer. "—we could take another look at the Morris house."

"It *is* a great house, the right size, and the price is good."

"You want to go back, tomorrow morning, say? I could call John Earle, see if he can meet us there. He's got friends in the construction business. We could ask for an estimate on the rooms you'll be needing right away."

"Let me sleep on it."

"I'd say take all the time you need, but, priced so low, somebody'll snap it up before you know it. I have another client at the college who's pretty taken with it."

"So, I have to decide quickly or run the risk of losing them both. I'd like to move in soon, so I can oversee the work, do some of it myself. I'm not bad with a paint brush." She paused and turned in the direction Mosey was waving.

"Hey, ladies," Robert said, walking up. "I see you've already ordered."

Mosey slid over. "Yeah, we have. We've had a long day."

Robert kissed Mosey on the cheek. "Hugh's coming. He stopped to speak to somebody at the bar. Shall we get a pitcher?"

"Fine with me," Lauren said.

As Robert looked for the waitress, Hugh's face appeared above the heads of a group gathered at the bar. "Over here," Robert called.

Hugh got to the booth, tossed his sports coat over the back, loosened his tie, and slid in next to Lauren. He slipped his arm around her shoulders and gave her a quick hug.

"I know." Lauren dropped her head. "Poor guy. It's pretty awful. But I'm okay," she said with a shrug—even if her expression suggested nothing of the kind.

Hugh looked across at Mosey. "Any word on the grisly incident?"

"Not yet. I suppose I should call Olivera. I'd like to know one way or the other."

"One way or the other what?" Robert asked as he returned to his seat.

"If Sunny Banks is off the market, temporarily."

"I'd imagine so," Robert said.

"Problem is," Mosey said, "we don't really know what happened, except that a body ended up in Martin Eldridge's car."

"You're cursed," Hugh said.

"Hey!" Mosey frowned at Hugh. "I am *not*. Or if I am, so are you."

"Every time Mosey lists a house," Hugh said to Lauren, "Robert and I end up digging up bones."

Miffy the waitress arrived, sparing him from having to substantiate his claim. "Here you go," she said, "a fresh pitcher of beer, mugs for the gents, and chips for the table. Anything else?"

"Miffy," Mosey said, "this is Dr. Lauren Wilson. She's new at the college. She's the new psychology professor."

"Nice to meet ya, ma'am," Miffy said. "You stick with these folks. They're some of the good 'uns."

"She didn't mean that," Hugh said. "She's angling for a big tip."

They all laughed, including Miffy, who waddled away toward the bar. "Let me know when you're ready for another pitcher," she called back.

"So, what's the plan?" Hugh poured a beer for Robert, then himself. "Have you seen anything you'd be ready to make an offer on?"

"I didn't care for the Stark house. Sunny Banks was my first choice, but now…"

Nobody said anything for a moment. The people at the next table were leaving and Mosey looked over. They were laughing, pulling out their change, piling it in the middle of the table. Now Miffy was back, clearing the table, scooping the change into her apron pocket. She balanced the tray on her hip and spritzed and wiped the table, then looked in Mosey's direction. "More chips?"

Mosey reached for a chip. "No, ma'am, we're good."

"Or maybe you want some chicken wings," she said as she approached. "Fried okra, fried pickles?" She set her tray down and pulled a menu from the waist of her apron. "Dr. Wilson, you want to see the menu? We've got a whole bunch of tasty appetizers." She placed the menu in front of Lauren.

"Thank you, Miffy." She opened the menu. "And you can call me Lauren. When I hear 'Dr. Wilson,' I start looking around for my mom."

"Now ain't that nice—your momma is a doctor, too."

"A medical doctor, a pediatrician."

"So I reckon you growed up healthy."

"You know what they say about the cobbler's children."

Miffy chuckled. "Yeah, I do."

"Lauren is from Philadelphia," Mosey said to Miffy.

"Philadelphia, Mississippi. I swanny, I got cousins over there."

"Pennsylvania," Mosey clarified.

Miffy looked perplexed. "How come you moving so far away? That's a good three-days' drive from here."

"Yes, actually it is, but I flew."

"I don't quite get all this movin' around." Miffy flashed her gray eyes at Lauren, then Hugh. "This 'un come here from far away, too."

Hugh intervened. "Miffy, I tell you what. Let's let Lauren sample some of our local specialties. Bring us a basket of fried okra."

"And chicken wings," Mosey chimed in, "with ranch dressing."

Miffy scribbled down the order. "That'll take about five, ten minutes. I'll bring it nice and hot." She winked at Lauren and waddled off.

"A little talkative but a sweet lady," Hugh said.

"You mentioned your mom's a doctor?" Robert said.

"Yeah, my dad, too."

"And siblings?" Robert said.

"Three older brothers."

"I don't see how your mom managed." Mosey reached for another chip, then passed the basket to Lauren.

"She didn't manage all that well."

On the verge of a chuckle, Mosey stopped. Lauren

looked dead serious—as did they all. Her inclination was to say something to brighten the mood, but she couldn't think of a thing. The day had had a doleful beginning, and the clouds wouldn't lift. She sipped her beer, letting her eyes wander around the room. She felt bad for Lauren. She'd counted on getting Sunny Banks. Doubtful now it'd pan out. Besides that, Lauren's apparent lack of pluck was a tad befuddling. Was she a person who couldn't deal with disappointment? She'd expected her to be pragmatic—like Eads or Carlotta.

Mosey, give the girl a break, for heaven's sake.

Mosey quashed a giggle.

Poet and don't know it.

"You're quiet." Hugh gave Mosey a little nudge under the table.

"Am I?"

They all were quiet, for a couple of minutes, till Miffy arrived with a tray of tasty-smelling morsels and began setting out saucers, ranch dressing, wings, and okra. "You ever tasted okra?" she said to Lauren.

"No, I haven't." Lauren raked a few pieces onto her plate.

"And try one of these." Miffy shook the basket of wings in her direction. "Uh-huh. It'll perk you right up."

Lauren added a wing to her plate.

"Makes you feel better about things, doesn't it, Miffy." Mosey took a wing and passed the basket to Robert and Hugh. "I think we're going to need another basket of these."

With a wink at Mosey, Miffy accepted the basket and headed back to the kitchen.

Chapter Nine

Mosey's Kitchen
Tuesday, November 3, 9:00 a.m.

It was early for a call, but Mosey phoned Nadia anyway. "I don't suppose I could convince you to take a few hours off to go exploring."

Robert, sitting across the table reading the paper, motioned with his thumb toward the kitchen door. Mosey stepped out on the landing, leaving the door ajar.

"Exploring where?" Nadia said.

It was a better answer than Mosey had anticipated, expecting a resounding "no." But, good, Nadia wasn't totally disinclined—at least that. "You remember that old bridle path that weaves through the properties along Little Smith?"

"Of course. Why?"

"Well, it's kind of a long story. I need to get over there soon as possible, but I'm not partial to going by myself."

"You thinking of hiking or riding?"

"Riding would be fun." Mosey glanced through the window at Robert.

"I tell you what," Nadia said. "I'll see if I can get a couple of horses from the stables. What time were you thinking?"

"Hey, if you can get horses, just say when."

"Okay, I'll call you back soon as I get a time."

Mosey stepped back in the kitchen and, picking up the breakfast platter, slid the last biscuit onto Robert's plate.

"Horseback riding?" He laid down the paper and, splitting open the biscuit, dribbled it with ribbon cane syrup. "Since when have you two done that?"

"It's been a while. What you got planned for the day?"

"We're picking up Lauren—" He took a bite and chewed. "—Hugh and I—and taking her wherever she wants to go."

"You expect she'll stick around past tomorrow?"

"She's got to get back to work, unless Olivera insists she stay, which seems pointless, if you ask me."

"I wonder if she's decided on a house. She said last evening she needed more time to think."

He unfolded the newspaper and, holding it up, pointed to a headline near the top. "Look at this. 'Body Found at Sunny Banks.' "

"I figured there would be something. Does it say anything we don't know?"

"They haven't been able to identify the body."

"Are they calling it a homicide?"

"Not yet. It says here—" He ran his index finger down the column. "—'Dr. Eads McGinnis of the Dent County Coroner's Office will determine cause of death once all tests are complete.' "

"So they *aren't* calling it a homicide."

"According to this."

"Huh." She piled the dishes in the sink and turned on the hot water. "I sure would like to know who the victim is." She washed and rinsed the platter and set it in the drain. "And why in the world the body was left in Old Man Eldridge's car."

"If you killed somebody, what would you do with the body?"

"That depends," she said with a grin. What a curious question for a husband to ask a wife.

"Of course, it *depends*—" He turned toward Mosey. "—but let's say in a case like this."

"Well…I suppose I'd get rid of it soon as possible, stash it far, far away if I could."

"So, then, why stash it in old Martin's Tyche?"

"The Eldridges aren't driving it. They've been out at the Magnolia for, good grief, six months? Nobody's been staying there as far as I know."

"Let's say the incident occurred at the house." He rocked back in his chair. "Why put the body in the car?"

"Better the car than the house. The house was soon to go on the market."

"Right, but it hadn't been listed, and the only one who knew the house was about to show was—"

"—whoever John Earle's been talking to about getting it listed."

"Exactly." He turned back to his plate and forked a bite of biscuit. "Anyone else would've figured the car was safe enough for the time being."

"No, I would never assume—"

"Well, whatever," Robert said, chewing. "Maybe you wouldn't, but that's not my point."

"But why put the body *inside* the car and not in the trunk?"

"You got me there." He wiped his mouth with his napkin and laid it next to his plate. "I can't see any practical reason, especially for putting it in the driver's seat. Seems darn inconvenient."

She dried her hands and pitched the towel under the sink. "But wait a minute—" She leaned against the counter. "—what if the perpetrator was planning on towing the car somewhere, making it look like an accident, maybe setting it on fire or rolling it down an embankment. If that was the plan," she said, eyes open wide, "the body would *need* to be in the driver's seat."

"That's right...but—" He raised a finger. "—how would it be explained that this unknown victim was driving Eldridge's car?"

"So maybe he stole it and, driving too fast, ran it off the road. If the car burned up or sank, that'd be the end of it. They'd never identify the body." She finished with a broad grin.

"Now, that last part," he said, "is unlikely. There'd be something left to identify the victim."

"Even if the car disintegrated?"

"Even if—"

"Yeah," she cut in, "I suppose if they could identify those bones in the cistern at Larkspur, they could identify a body that hadn't been dead long."

"But the advantage would be to get rid of the evidence. Fire or water would seriously degrade most anything."

"What I'd like to know is why there? Why Sunny Banks? Either the perpetrator or the victim had some connection with the house or the Eldridges."

"Which is all the more reason," he said, "for the perpetrator to want to get the body *away* from the house. And he could have done that if you and Lauren hadn't shown up."

"That gives me the creeps." Shivering, she rubbed

her arms. "You think the killer was ready to get the car out of there, and then we popped in?"

"I wouldn't be surprised. Or maybe that's not it at all. Maybe there was another reason."

"Like what?"

"I don't know," he said with a shrug. "Maybe he needed to be somewhere, and it would have looked suspicious if he hadn't shown up."

"Or maybe none of it was planned," she said, "and he had to figure out how to tow the car away. Or maybe he just needed to think, come up with a plan."

"Yeah, a plan. Highly unlikely he had one, not from the start. If the person had planned the murder—if it was a murder—he'd have made arrangements to move the body, at the very least have a body bag on hand. He could have put the body in his vehicle and taken off—" He stared into space. "—buried it, dumped it in the river. The levee's no more than a couple of miles from there. Or, for heaven's sake—" He threw out a hand. "—there're a dozen creeks and ponds around there. People dump stuff all the time. Maybe not bodies…"

She thought about that as she paced from the counter to the window and back. "You're right. Unlikely it was planned."

"But listen to me, Mosey—" He stood, fishing in his pocket for his keys. "—you stay out of this, you hear?"

"You sound like Daddy."

"Ellis was a wise man."

"Yeah—" She nodded. "—he was."

Later that morning, on their way to the stables, Mosey and Nadia hashed out the preliminaries. They would ride along Little Smith, then take Sunny Banks Cutoff to the bridle path that ran along the river a short distance from the houses. Sunny Banks and a few of the older homes were on the far end of what was now called Cottonwood Acres, where Hembree's nouveaux riches—towboat people included—had built their pricey homes.

The sky was blue and striped with white clouds. Mosey's horse was a sorrel, gentle and well trained. He seemed like a happy horse—his lower jaw was loose and his nostrils, soft and relaxed. She gave him a good pat on the neck, then, put her foot in the stirrup and, holding on to the saddle horn, pulled herself up. Nadia's horse, a little skittish, was a hearty thoroughbred, a recycled race horse she herself had trained for falconry.

"You ever go hunting anymore?" Mosey asked.

Nadia shook her head. "That's why Legend's at the stables. He needs to be ridden."

They went along at a walk. When a slight wind blew up, Mosey lifted her hoodie over her head. "I know that old bridle path has got to be here somewhere."

"Hope so," Nadia said. "It was a lovely place to wander."

"Yeah, it was. Reckon we'll come to it if we head toward the river?"

"Maybe, but we could miss it if we don't aim far enough south."

"Yeah, it meanders around, sort of like the river." Mosey pulled back gently on the reins, bringing her horse to a halt. "Whoa, Molly." She looked around. "Seems like it was south of the Square. I was thinking about that map Rafael's great-grandfather made. I don't suppose it had a detail on it like the bridle path, you reckon?"

"I saw it just that one time at the Tavernette," Nadia

said, "when we were looking at the area around Larkspur."

"Well, Larkspur isn't that far from here, but north, right?"

"I'm thinking Larkspur is over there, and Sunny Banks, over there. The bridle path pretty much follows the levee."

"I don't remember it being that close," Mosey said. "It's too marshy for a bridle path. You ever see a horse get stuck in mud?"

"Good grief, Mosey. Why'd you put that image in my head?"

"Sorry, I was just remembering—"

"Never mind. Let's think positive. Let's imagine ourselves finding what we came to find." She pressed her calves against the horse and moved forward. "And what would that be, by the way?"

"Well, a couple of things, like what made 'em name the place 'Sunny Banks'?"

"You got me."

"There must be some body of water on the property, wouldn't you think?"

"Possibly, but what's that got to do with the incident?"

"We were talking it over this morning—Robert and I. Maybe the perpetrator planned to tow the car away, make it look like an accident. Roll it down a creek bank or set it on fire. Either way, there'd hardly be any evidence left to tie him to the crime."

"Mosey, you're grabbing at straws."

"I am not," Mosey snapped, "and it would have worked if Lauren and I hadn't showed up when we did."

"How long had he been dead?"

"I don't know." Mosey was staring down at her horse instead of looking straight ahead. "The paper didn't say, but you know what I just realized?"

"Watch out, Mosey," Nadia called out.

"What?"

"You were heading straight for that limb."

"I was not." She sat up high in the saddle. "So what'd you realize?"

"Jack Eldridge—he's the one that contacted John Earle."

"You're not suggesting—"

"He knew the house was about to show."

"I wouldn't go around saying that if I were you."

"Nadia, for Pete's sake. You're as bad as Robert. I would *never* start such a rumor."

"Have you talked to Olivera?" Nadia said, changing the subject.

"Briefly. He wanted more information about the listing. I imagine he'll be in touch again."

"Why would he want to talk to *you*?"

"I guess 'cause I discovered the body."

"He'd sooner offer his hand to a rattlesnake, if you ask me."

"Nadia," Mosey yelped. "Did you have to mention snakes?"

Nadia chortled. "There aren't any snakes around here, not in November."

"Huh, I wouldn't count on it."

"But go back to what you were saying," Nadia said, "about you and Lauren foiling the perpetrator's plans."

"Yeah, so we figure that's why the body was in the car."

"Safe assumption."

"Besides that, it narrows down the suspects."

"How's that?"

"The perp must have *something* to do with the house."

"Possibly," Nadia said.

"Otherwise, what was he doing there?"

"Maybe it was the victim who was connected."

"Could be. Surely one of them was."

"Well, I don't know much about Sunny Banks," Nadia said.

"That's what we're doing here now. The owners are out at Magnolia. And as far as the house is concerned, it's going on the market any day."

"It's not already on the market?"

"Not yet. John Earle's waiting for the papers to come in, but, since I had a client who was interested..."

"How'd she hear about it?"

"When she first asked about it, I just assumed—"

"What?"

"—that somebody had told her about it or maybe she'd seen a picture on the Hembree website. It *is* a historic home. But yesterday she said she'd met somebody at the Tavernette bar when she was here for her interview."

"And?"

"He told her about the Historic District, but then said he liked the properties on the outskirts better."

"Who was it?"

"I have no idea. Didn't want to pry."

"Hmm. You think she knows more than she's saying?"

Mosey shrugged.

"Sounds suspicious to me," Nadia said.

"You're *naturally* suspicious."

"It pays to be suspicious."

"I guess, in the antique business, it would."

"You'd better believe it."

"Did I tell you," Mosey said, "we were thinking this might not be an actual murder?"

"How you figure?"

"Maybe the victim fell, hit his head, and whoever found the body—"

"Oh, my goodness!" Nadia steered her horse sharply to the left. "Would you look at that?"

They'd come up on a stand of tupelos, or blackgums as locals called them, that had sprinkled their yellow leaves over the bog and surrounding banks. In the rays of the morning sun, the banks gleamed as if covered in a mantle of gold coins.

"Sunny banks!" Mosey yelled.

"Indeed," Nadia said, "a sight to behold."

Chapter Ten

Police Station
November 3, 10:00 a.m.

Monday night before he left the station, Olivera had phoned John Earle Shepherd, and they'd agreed to meet the following morning.

"Mr. Shepherd, thanks for coming in." Olivera gestured toward the metal folding chair next to his desk.

Shepherd obliged and sat hunched over, elbows on his thighs, as if ready to bolt at the least provocation. "What's this about, Lieutenant?"

Olivera pushed a manila folder toward Shepherd but didn't open it, just sat tapping it with his pen. "I guess you know a body was found at Sunny Banks yesterday around noon."

"I heard."

"I suppose Ms. Frye told you."

"She did." He nodded.

"I understand you have direct contact with the owners."

"That's right."

Olivera stretched back. "We don't have much to go on so far. We haven't been able to identify the victim."

"I see." Shepherd sat up straight, brow raised.

"But the car belongs to Martin Eldridge Sr.," Olivera continued, "former resident of Sunny Banks.

Have you been in touch with him?"

"Oh, no, Martin's not in touch with much of anybody."

"And his wife?"

Shepherd relaxed back. "Far as I know, she's out at the Magnolia with him. Both are quite elderly."

"If you don't mind my asking, who's involved in the sale?" Olivera pulled his tablet out of the desk drawer.

"Of the house?"

Olivera nodded.

"I was contacted by their attorney."

"Who would be…?"

"Carlotta Humphrey."

"I suppose, then, she's the one I ought to be talking to." Olivera scribbled down her name, though it was unlikely he'd forget. Carlotta was anything but forgettable. "But while I've got you here, would you take a look at the post-mortem photographs?" He put down his pen and opened the folder.

"Certainly, if it would help you get started on the case." He glanced at the open folder. "It behooves us to see this thing straightened out soon as possible, so we can list the property. It'll list as stigmatized at any rate, but if the crime's solved, all the better."

"I see your point." He placed a photograph on the desk in front of Shepherd.

Shepherd slipped on his readers and leaned forward. "He looks familiar, I'll grant you that." He angled the photograph toward the light. "But I can't say for sure."

"What about this one?" He handed him a second photograph. "Any better?"

Shepherd leaned forward again. "I can't tell you his name, but, again, he looks familiar."

Olivera put the photographs back in the folder and set it aside. "I'll speak to Ms. Humphrey about the property, but if I could bother you with a couple of things. Do you happen to have any personal history with the Eldridges? I was wondering, since they approached you personally about selling the house."

"Personal history?" He sat back and crossed his legs. "I've known the Eldridges pretty much all my life, but not well."

"Could you elaborate?"

"The Eldridge kids were in school with me—Jack, mostly. He's about my age. A few years older."

"Are you still in touch with him?"

"Not so much since he moved to Vicksburg. The Eldridges are in the towboat business. I guess you know that."

"The towboat business," Olivera repeated.

"Yeah, a good many people around here moved away when Vicksburg became the new hub. But I've never been involved in the river. My family has always been in property mostly and farming some."

For Olivera, that was a new wrinkle on the face of Hembree's social system. Farmer or boatman. One or the other. "Did Jack take over the business when his father retired?"

"I'm sure he did, but like I said, I haven't kept up with the Eldridges that much. I run into Jack at the hunting club now and again."

So, apparently, boatmen hunted, too, though the image hadn't quite materialized for him. He'd figured they fished, frog gigged, hunted duck, but he hadn't imagined a boatman in the woods, rifle in hand, poised to take down a big buck. Seemed like everybody hunted, or at least that was the way it was sounding to him. "So you've seen him more or less recently, in the last few months, say."

"I saw him at the start of dove season, in September that would have been."

"He didn't happen to mention that he was selling Sunny Banks, did he?"

"He might have mentioned it. But we haven't talked since then. Like I said before, more recently, it was Carlotta who contacted me about the listing, though Jack might have said something at one time."

"Anything else about the Eldridges you can tell me?"

"Lieutenant, you think they had something to do with this murder?"

"Now, I didn't say it was a murder."

"What do you suspect? An accident of some kind?"

"Could have been an accident." Olivera rolled back from his desk and stood.

"You think he fell, hit his head?" Shepherd stood, too.

"At this point, anything is possible."

Olivera extended his hand, thanked Shepherd for coming in, then, walked him to the front of the office. On his way back to his cubicle, he picked up a cup of coffee and, seated again at his desk, called for Springer.

The burly redhead poked his head around the door of the partition. "Yes, Chief."

"Does it seem strange to you that boatmen hunt?"

"Not really, everybody hunts."

"Surely not everybody."

"Women don't hunt, well, not much. Some of the younger ones do."

"I heard Nadia Abboud hunts," Olivera said.

"Yeah, she's a special case, hunts with a falcon."

"Huh." He turned toward his desk. "Get Dot Cowsley on the phone, would you? See if Carlotta can squeeze me in this morning or, if not, this afternoon."

"Sure, Chief." Springer disappeared beyond the partition.

"Dot," Olivera heard him say, "this is Sergeant Springer. Lieutenant Olivera would like to speak to Ms. Humphrey, soon as possible. ... Un-huh, un-huh, I see. Hold on a second, please, ma'am." He reappeared at the door. "Chief, she can squeeze you in right now if you can get over there. But Carlotta's got an appointment in half an hour, so it'd have to be right now."

"Tell her I'm on my way." He slid the folder with the photographs into his briefcase, slung his sports coat over his shoulder, and crossed the office. "Ms. Hill, I'll be at Ms. Humphrey's office for the next half hour. Then I'm grabbing a bite to eat, but call me if you hear anything from Dr. McGinnis."

She scratched down his instructions on a sticky note and pressed it against her phone. "I got it, Lieutenant."

"Ms. Hill, you don't hunt, do you?"

She scrunched her nose. "No, but why do you ask?"

"Nothing, just wondered."

The walk from the station to the Square was long enough for Olivera to put his wits together but not long enough to put them together satisfactorily. He hadn't anticipated getting to see Carlotta so quickly. With more time, he might have figured out exactly what he wanted and how to get it. No doubt, she was the town's most clued-up lawyer. Her stepfather and stepbrother, Amos and Ellis Frye, had schooled her properly, though her familiarity with the citizenry of Hembree didn't quite match theirs—or so he'd been told. But now that Carlotta was at the helm, she'd acquired a good bit of expertise on her own. In his year and a half in Hembree, he'd come to the conclusion that if anybody knew Hembree like the back of their hand, it was she. And what she hadn't learned from her predecessors or on her own, she could access by way of the firm's big archive. She was the sphinx at the door, though not a particularly foreboding sphinx, he'd decided.

He tramped up the stairs and after ringing the doorbell, entered the outer office, where Dot stood with a hefty stack of files balanced on her arm. "Lieutenant, you made it over so fast." She set down the files and came toward him. "May I take your hat?"

He handed it over with a smile.

"Hey, that's a new one," she said admiringly. "Mr. Frye, Mr. *Ellis* Frye, preferred a fedora, too, though his wife was forever buying him trilbies." She placed the hat on the rack. "And let me get you a cup of coffee. Want a cup? I've got a fresh pot."

As Dot rattled on, he stood nodding and smiling. "I think I'll pass, but thank you, ma'am. Is Ms. Humphrey with someone now?" He glanced toward the open door.

"No, you go right on in. She's expecting you." She pushed back her cuff and checked her watch. "She's got half an hour, maybe a little less, before her next appointment. "Go right in."

He tapped lightly on the doorframe and looked in. "Dot said I could see you now?"

Carlotta, staring down at a document, looked up and slipped off her readers. "Lieutenant, come on in. I don't have much time, but Dot said it sounded urgent. Have a seat." She flicked a hand toward the upholstered chairs set around a low mahogany table.

"It's urgent, uh," he said, "but to be completely honest, I'm not sure we've got a crime here, at least not yet." He'd learned that opening up to Carlotta was an excellent primer for getting her to open up to him.

"Not sure you've got a crime?" she repeated.

"The victim may have fallen," he said, sitting, "or I guess it's possible he was bludgeoned across the back of the head. I'm waiting on Dr. McGinnis to give us cause of death. But here's the thing."

Before he got to say what *the thing* was, she sat down in the chair nearest his and scooted toward him. "I'm going to guess you're talking about the body found at Sunny Banks."

"Yes."

"And somebody's told you I'm the Eldridges' attorney." She set her readers on the table and placed her hands around her knees.

"Right on both counts. I spoke with John Earle Shepherd just now. He told me what he knew, but thought you would know more about the sale."

"He's right. They've asked me to handle the sale of the house and the car, Mr. Eldridge's car."

"The car the body was found in, I'm guessing."

She nodded. "So, how can I help?"

"First—" He cleared his throat. "—the victim didn't have any identification, and we can't get a fingerprint match off the data base. Looks like whoever stuffed him in the driver's seat didn't want anybody to know who he was. So, if you wouldn't mind taking a look at the post-mortem photographs…" He pulled the folder from his briefcase and placed both shots of the victim on the table.

She looked at one, then, the other, then, the first one again. "I don't know him."

"Doesn't even look familiar?"

"Not really." She studied them again before saying, "Not a face you'd remember. Nothing memorable about it, though he is—was—fairly attractive. But the features, the hair, they're all sort of cookie-cutter, wouldn't you say?"

"Cookie-cutter?"

"Ordinary…white Anglo-Saxon Protestant, which is the *minority* around here. There's nothing exotic, nothing ethnic. I'll tell you one thing about river towns, Lieutenant, since you're a recent import." She looked up. "And don't take offense, but most of us Hembreeites look *something*. African American, Chinese, Lebanese, Italian, Irish, whatever." She laid the pictures in front of him and twisted them around. "Look at the nose. If he were from any of the lines I've mentioned, his nose would be more distinctive. That's just a plain nose." She pointed. "See what I mean?"

He blinked a couple of times.

"What color were his eyes?" she asked.

"Blue."

"See, I could have guessed that."

He slid the photographs back into the folder. "Okay, so we don't have here a memorable face or an ethnic face, but what we do have is someone who, in all likelihood, was connected to the Eldridges. I know it's a leap, but I'm willing to take it, at least for now. I'm hoping Dr. McGinnis will come up with something. But in the meantime, can you give me any tips about the Eldridges' associates, someone, say, who might have had reason to be on the property? Or, of course, this person could have been related to the Eldridges."

Carlotta inhaled deeply. "Wow, Lieutenant, that's a big order."

"How so?"

"Eldridge and Son is a big operation. You know they're in the towboat business. Not here anymore. They moved the office long time ago, before my time. But, of course, I've got the archive."

"Let's not get into that quite yet. Tell me—do any transactions or conflicts of a business or personal nature stand out in your mind?"

She shifted in her seat. "I'd be glad to help if I could, but I wouldn't feel right about getting into anything legal, wouldn't want to reveal anything unnecessarily. You understand."

"Of course." He slid the folder into his briefcase and zipped it. "Just one last question. Could you tell me who you've been in touch with about the property?"

"Jack Eldridge spoke with me about getting the house on the market."

"Was all that by phone? He hasn't driven over from Vicksburg?"

"I can't be sure where he was phoning from. I assumed he was in Vicksburg. Otherwise, he probably would have dropped by."

"And was he the one you and Shepherd contacted about getting permission for Ms. Frye to show the house?"

"I'm not sure who exactly gave permission. I got an email from his secretary, so I guess it was Jack."

"And this woman," he continued, "who saw the house, Dr. Lauren Wilson. Know anything about her?" He stood, preparing to leave.

Carlotta shook her head. "Not a thing, Lieutenant. Should I?"

Chapter Eleven

Morgue, Delta Infirmary
November 3, 12:00 noon

On the way down the stairs from Carlotta's office, Olivera phoned his sergeant. "Springer, did you get the evidence over to the morgue?"

"Yes, Chief. Hold on a second, would you?"

"Sure." He leaned against the side of the building, briefcase clutched under his arm. No one was on his side of the Square. They were all on the other side, lined up at the Tavernette. He'd missed his chance for a quick lunch.

"Sorry, Chief. What was that?"

"The evidence, Springer. What'd you get?"

"The usual. *Crunch, crunch.* Fibers, hairs, and a sample of the blood, of course. *Crunch, crunch.*" Springer paused to swallow.

"Springer, would you cool it with the chips?"

"Sorry, Chief."

"You find any blood anywhere else, other than the front seat?"

"Nope. The back seat and trunk were clean."

"Find anything else?"

"A spare tire and some tools—that was it."

Olivera thought for a minute. "So, nothing in the glove compartment?"

"Just the manual."

"No registration?"

"Nope."

"Okay. You and Reagan are heading out to the property, right?"

"Just about, soon as we finish lunch. We'll get it cordoned off and check the back section. That's what you wanted us to do, isn't it?"

"Yeah, and see if you can find any interesting landmarks back there, any reason to call it Sunny Banks." He clicked off.

Deciding to skip lunch, Olivera picked up the squad car at the station and drove to the infirmary. When he reached the morgue, he paused at the door, pulling his thoughts together before going in. "Good afternoon, Dr. McGinnis. You're up to the usual, I see." He tossed his new fedora toward the antique hat rack in the corner beyond the door.

"You're getting pretty good at that, Lieutenant." She smiled briefly, then looked back at the corpse of John Doe. A sheet covered most of the body, leaving only the head exposed. She pulled the sheet over the head and stepped back.

He glanced toward the counter where a couple of packets and corked vials were spread out on a white cloth. "The evidence Springer brought over—was it helpful?" He felt under the upper cabinet for the switch and turned on the light.

"It could be helpful," she said. "I haven't had a chance to examine it all."

"He didn't get very much, did he?"

She shrugged. "Some kind of ID would have been helpful. Without that, we might have to take the DNA route. I've made x-rays of his teeth. I'll get them out to the local dentists this afternoon."

"What about the hair?"

"I wanted to show you that." Her eyebrows lifted. "It's sort of curious. I was looking at samples of the known hair—the victim's hair—and comparing them with the hair Springer brought in, the victim's, maybe, or possibly the assailant's." Stepping to the counter, she placed a slide under the comparison microscope and adjusted the magnification. "Take a look." She waved him over. "Tell me what you see."

He situated himself in front of the microscope. "Two similar hairs." He looked back at McGinnis.

"The basic identifications are very close. Hair varies a lot, even when it's taken from the same person. Variation can occur even along the shaft. And given all that, the similarities are striking."

"So, what are you saying?" He leaned against the counter.

"I'm not saying anything conclusive, but it's my guess that if we send the hair of both individuals out for DNA analysis, well, it wouldn't surprise me if the victim and the suspect are related."

"But we aren't sure the unknown hair is *from* the suspect, are we?"

"No, it could be from someone else. But the unknown hair—some of it—is stained with the victim's blood, and that narrows it down a little."

Olivera rubbed his chin. "We'll take all the help we can get at this point. By the way, speaking of grabbing at straws," he said as he paced away from the counter, "I spoke to Carlotta Humphrey just now. Turns out she's the Eldridges' lawyer, which isn't a surprise. I thought she might be able to tell me something about the sale of the property."

"Could she?"

"Not that much, but she said Jack Eldridge, the elderly couple's son, was her contact. He or maybe his secretary gave permission for Ms. Frye to show the property."

"I guess you need to speak to him." She sat on the stool next to her desk.

"Yeah, and that might mean driving to Vicksburg. He moved down there some years ago."

"It's not far, about forty miles. It's a pretty drive if you take the river route."

Olivera tapped his forehead with the heel of his hand.

"What?" she asked.

"I forgot to ask Carlotta about the keys to the Tyche—who has them."

"Jack Eldridge, wouldn't you think?"

"Probably, unless he has a contact here in town, somebody who looks after things." He moved to her desk and, perching on the edge, said, "By the way, I don't guess you'd happen to know the Eldridges."

"Not really, but my parents did. They're part of the same generation."

"You have any impression of who they are, I mean, what kind of people they are?"

"My parents didn't care much for Jack."

"Why's that?"

"Daddy isn't one to offer opinions about people. My mother, on the other hand, made it clear she didn't care for him."

"Anything specific?"

"She thought he was a womanizer. Of course, she didn't use that word."

"What word *did* she use?"

"She said he was a lady's man."

"Ha, nice euphemism. You don't hear that anymore."

"Nope."

"Any chance of rushing the DNA?"

"I can try."

"You know, something else has been bugging me."

"What's that?"

"Lauren Wilson."

She didn't respond, just wrinkled her nose.

"How did she know about Sunny Banks?" he continued. "Technically, it wasn't on the market. She came from Philadelphia to see it. She looked at a couple of other houses, but, according to Ms. Frye, this was the one she wanted."

"Maybe she heard about it when she came for her interview."

"Yes, must have. I ought to call Ms. Frye, see what she knows about that. By the way, Carlotta said she didn't think John Doe here had a memorable face."

She moved back to the gurney and lifted the sheet. "He has a handsome face. Youngish, pleasant, but I'd agree. No distinguishing features except maybe his teeth."

Curiosity piqued, Olivera approached the gurney. "What about his teeth?"

She slipped on gloves and pulled back the victim's lips. He had perfectly straight teeth but with unusually pointed cuspids. "Not many people have that. Otherwise, he has a fine set of teeth, not a single filling."

Olivera lowered his brow. "You aren't suggesting he's from a long line of vampires, are you?"

"No, silly." She laughed.

"Whew. That's a relief. Okay, Mr. John Doe, who are you? It's as if you didn't want us to know. No ID, a handsome face but no distinguishing characteristics except a couple of spiky canines. Hmm. Nobody around here knows you. I wonder if Jack Eldridge knows you. He should, you were in his father's car." He looked at McGinnis. "I guess I'm going to Vicksburg."

Chapter Twelve

Wednesday, November 4, 7:30 a. m.
Road to Vicksburg, MS

The night before, when Olivera had left the station around six, he hadn't heard back from Springer and Reagan. The next morning, before he took off for Vicksburg, he gave Springer a call. "Morning, Springer. You find anything yesterday?"

"No, Chief. Reagan hit a metal trap and tore his front tire all to pieces."

"Sounds like somebody's been doing some illegal trapping. Did you see anything at all—tracks, blood?"

"We didn't get very far, Chief. Where we were, there was just that old bridle path, lots of trees, leaves turnin' and all that. I imagine it'd be worth another trip. Like I said, we didn't get very far. But we did cordon off the house like you said."

"Okay. I'm driving over to Vicksburg to see what I can find out about the Eldridges. And while I'm gone, I want you and Reagan to try again. Check out the house, too. See if you can get Mosey Frye to let you in. She has the key, at least she did. If she doesn't, I imagine Ms. Smiley knows who does. Yeah, give Ms. Smiley a call first. And check the jimmy marks on the windowsill. Mosey mentioned she saw some marks on one of the windows on the side of the living room closest to the garage."

"Sure thing, Chief. We'll start with the house if we can get in, then scour that whole back section. We'll come up with somethin', don't you worry."

"One more thing. Let Ms. Hill know where I am, and remind her, if she gets a report from the coroner's office, to give me a call. I talked to Dr. McGinnis yesterday, and I'm hoping she might have something today. You got all that?"

"Yeah, I got it, Chief. By the way, I don't suppose you'll be having lunch at the Plantation Tea Room."

"Where the devil is the Plantation Tea Room?"

"Oh, it's a fine place to stop for lunch. Right there on the outskirts of town. You can't miss it. And, on the off chance you stop, would you mind picking up some pecan pralines?"

"Sure, Springer. I'll make it a point." Olivera laughed, shook his head, and clicked off.

He took Little Smith south and connected with Highway 65 toward Vicksburg. Eads had been right in telling him to take the river road. The river's old course flowed serenely along the left side of the road. Ferns and overhanging trees, some of them cypresses, grew along the banks, which were green and neatly kept. An occasional pecan orchard flashed by, trees loaded down with pecans. "Pecan pralines, indeed," he muttered, then laughed. "Must be in the DNA around here."

At Interstate 20 past Tallulah, he crossed the Mississippi River bridge, but, not seeing any sign of the Plantation Tea Room—and it wasn't lunchtime anyway—he decided to catch it on the way back. As he approached Vicksburg, he wasn't sure how to get to the Eldridge business and pulled off at a service station. He motioned, and a man approached the window. "Could you tell me how to get to Eldridge and Son?"

"You follow I-20 East across the bridge," the man said, pointing, "till you come to the Waffle House on the other side. There's a street right there, Warrenton Street, and you turn to the left onto Washington and follow it past the casinos. You'll see it on the right, Eldridge and Son Barge Lines. There's no big sign or nothin', just a long, white building."

Olivera thanked the attendant. He pulled back onto the highway and, following the man's directions, soon arrived at his destination. Like the man had said, there wasn't a big sign, just a white building with a small parking area and, across from the other side of the building, the Mississippi River. He climbed the steps, looking around for the front door but, not finding it, followed the veranda to the other side, where he came to a large, double glass door with Eldridge and Son Barge Lines spelled out in gold-trimmed letters. He opened the door halfway and spoke to the woman at reception. "I assume I've come to the right place."

"Well, that depends." She got up from her desk. "What are you looking for? This is Eldridge and Son Barge Lines."

He nodded and entered.

"Do you have an appointment?"

"I don't." He held out his badge and identification.

"I see. I expect you want to see Mr. Eldridge. He's the president of the company."

"Yes, Mr. Jack Eldridge."

"Have a seat." She gestured toward a captain's chair in the corner next to the door.

He sat and, slipping his identification back into his

breast pocket, looked around the room. There were pictures of towboats—a dozen or more—and men, some in suits, some in work clothes, in groups of two or three, arms stretched around one another's shoulders. They looked to him like a tight bunch. His only encounter with boatmen (when a towboat sank near the Greenville Bridge and the Coast Guard asked for help from nearby agencies) had taught him just how tight they could be. He got up and ambled over to the centerpiece of the picture display, a portrait of a man he took to be the individual known in Hembree as Old Man Eldridge, founder of the company. A brass plate on the frame confirmed his deduction—"In Honor of Martin J. Eldridge Sr."

"Mr. Eldridge can see you now." The secretary pointed over her shoulder. "It's the office at the end of the hall."

On his way down the hall, he passed more pictures of boats and boatmen before coming to an open door. "Mr. Jack Eldridge?" He showed his identification to a man seated at a large wooden desk. "Lieutenant Olivera of the Hembree, Arkansas Police Department."

Eldridge raised slightly out of his chair. "You're out of your jurisdiction, aren't you, Lieutenant?" With a gesture of his hand, he offered Olivera a seat. "What brings you to Vicksburg?"

"I thought by now you might have heard." He slipped his shield into his pocket.

"Naw." His ruddy complexion turned brighter.

"I thought maybe Ms. Humphrey contacted you."

"You mean Carlotta?" He shook his head. "Naw."

Olivera hadn't given much thought to what the president of Eldridge and Son might look like, though he'd gotten it in his head he might look a little like John Doe. Must have been what McGinnis had said about the similarity of the *known* and *unknown* hair. Eldridge had a nice head of hair for his age—late fifties, he figured—dark like the victim's, streaks of gray at the temples. His features were ordinary—what Carlotta would have called cookie cutter—with the exception of his eyes, which were translucent blue and lined with dark lashes.

"Have a seat, Lieutenant."

Olivera sat and placed his briefcase on his lap. "There was an incident at your parents' house in Hembree."

"What kind of incident?" He reached for a package of cigarettes, shook out a couple, and offered one to Olivera.

"No, thanks," he said and continued. "We found a body in the Tyche-XL500 parked in the garage at Sunny Banks. To be more precise, it was the real estate agent, Ms. Frye, Ms. Mosey Frye, who discovered the body. She happened to go into the garage and saw the body slumped over the steering wheel."

Eldridge snapped open his lighter and lit the cigarette. "I haven't heard a word."

"So you haven't spoken to Ms. Humphrey?"

"Not this week," he said, exhaling. "I did get a call from John Earle about showing the house. I told my secretary to tell him it was okay."

"If you wouldn't mind taking a look at a post-mortem photograph of the victim." Olivera took the folder out of his briefcase. "It'd be helpful if we could get an ID on the man."

Eldridge picked up the front pose, then, the profile. He shook his head. "I don't know him. Looks like a young fellow."

"Well, he's not that young," Olivera said, "probably late thirties, according to the coroner."

"What was he doing at Sunny Banks, you reckon?"

Olivera gave a half laugh. "If only we knew. The evidence is pretty thin. I was hoping you might be able to help us out. The only connection we can draw is with your family or the family business."

He shook his head and took a puff off his cigarette. "We hire a good many workers. Some of our Hembree people moved here with us."

"You're sure he never worked for your company?"

"The captains have more contact with the men than I do. He could have worked for us briefly, and I might not recognize him."

"Any chance I could speak to your captains?"

"Sure, but there's a bunch of 'em. It'd be easier if we faxed 'em a picture. About half are on the river, either this one, the Tennessee, or the Ohio. Mary at the front desk could take care of that."

"I'd appreciate it."

"Hold on a second." He picked up the receiver and punched in a number. "Mary, I need you to make some copies." He hung up. "She'll be right in."

Mary poked her head in the door, and Eldridge handed her the photographs. "Copy these, both of them, and send them to the captains. Tell them we need an identification."

"ASAP?" she asked.

He nodded.

"So this brings me to my next question," Olivera said. "I asked Ms. Humphrey about this, but she didn't feel like she was at liberty to say. Has your company been involved in any kind of conflict recently, say in the last year or two?"

"Conflict." Eldridge chuckled. "You must not know much about the towboat business. We've got some kind of conflict going on most the time. Nothing that big, mind you. Just little disputes here and there."

"What sort of disputes?"

"Environmental, personnel, little stuff. The lawyers handle it."

"Like Ms. Humphrey?"

"That depends. Carlotta has more to do with the family. Our lawyers here in Vicksburg deal with the business."

"But with Sunny Banks being in Hembree, she'd take care of anything related to the property?"

Eldridge nodded.

Mary came back in with Olivera's pictures.

"We'll send those photographs out today," Eldridge said. "We'll let you know if anyone recognizes him."

Olivera stood. "By the way, does the name Lauren Wilson mean anything to you?"

"Lauren Wilson," he repeated. "Is she from around here?"

"No, she's from Philadelphia. She was with the real estate agent when the body was discovered. She's the one interested in Sunny Banks."

"Huh. Why would a woman from Philadelphia be interested in Sunny Banks?"

Olivera was tempted to say "good question," but he didn't. "My understanding is she has taken a position at Blanchard College and is looking for a fixer-upper."

"Plenty of those in Hembree. Isn't Sunny Banks big for a single woman?"

"I'm not sure she *is* single."

"Oh, I suppose not." He turned red. He had the kind of skin that blushed easily.

"Well, thanks, Mr. Eldridge." Olivera extended a hand. "I'll leave my card with the lady at the front desk. Please don't hesitate to call if you think of something."

Chapter Thirteen

November 4, 8:00 a.m.
Sunny Banks Woods

Reagan rapped his knuckles against the windshield of the SUV. "Are we taking rifles, ammo?"

Springer rolled down the window. "You got your gun, ain't ya?"

"Yeah, I got my gun."

"That oughta be enough." Springer sighed. For certain, it was enough, but Reagan was just that way, wasn't he? Always wantin' to make a mountain out of a dang mole hill.

Reagan slid into the passenger seat, and Springer pulled out. He looked both ways and cruised off toward Little Smith. "The chief's countin' on us to scour the woods, bring back anything suspicious. You ever hunt the woods around Sunny Banks?"

"Sure fire. You'd be surprised what you run into," Reagan said. "Bears—" His eyes bugged out. "—wild boar. There's no tellin'—"

"You ever shoot a wild boar?" Springer interrupted.

"Are you kiddin' me? I wouldn't subject my dogs to that kind of ruckus." Reagan's brows knitted into a frown. "Wild boar's about the worst thing in the woods except snakes. You ever run up on a nest of cotton-mouths?"

"Can't say that I have, but I've heard stories," Springer said. "Everybody around here's got more dang snake tales." He pursed his lips, slowly shook his head. "I grew up hearing all about snake *nests*."

"You sound like you don't believe in 'em." Reagan's body stiffened. "I'm telling ya, the *Gazette* had a story not so long ago about a water skier fell in a nest of snakes. He had two dozen or more bites. Two dozen *or more*. It was in the paper, I'm telling ya."

"Well, if it was in the paper..." Springer said, his head spiraling down toward his shoulders, but Reagan went right on, unaltered by his sarcasm.

"Yeah, we got all kinds of snakes, some of them poisonous. Not much talk about 'em this time of year. They're around, though, and you'd do well to remember that."

"You ever run up on a copperhead?" Springer said.

"Lots of times." Reagan said it with a shrug, as if any fool knew that.

"What about an alligator?" Springer thought he might as well raise the stakes.

"Well, not in the woods, but you start wading around in the swampy bottoms, and you're bound to see one. Bound to. I tell you one thing." Reagan poked the air with his index finger. "I gave up frog giggin' because of an alligator. Flopped over in the boat with us, and my daddy grabbed him around the middle and stood him straight up, whilst my brother and me stabbed the daylights out of the critter. You've never seen such a bloody mess in all your life." He chuckled.

"Where was that?"

"Lake Eileen, that little lake on the other side of Lake Lafayette." Reagan lowered his head and looked out the side window. "Hey, there it is, right there."

"What?"

"The bridle path. Aren't we looking for the bridle path?"

Springer slowed down and pulled off the road.

"You want your hip boots, Springer?" Reagan said, getting out.

"Naw, it's pretty dry around here."

"I'm putting on mine. Open the tailgate, would you?"

Springer hit the release and stepped out.

"You just watch," Reagan said. "Soon as we start aiming down toward the river, we'll hit some swampy spots."

"Well, I guess I might as well have mine, too. Hand them over here, would you?"

They propped themselves against the SUV and stepped into their hip boots.

"We don't need no camo, I guess," Reagan said.

"Not unless you're hoping to kill a deer." Springer rolled his eyes.

"I don't expect the lieutenant would appreciate us turning this into a huntin' trip." Reagan laughed.

They followed the bridle path south and before long came to the place that had given the Eldridge house its name. "That is about the prettiest thing I've ever seen," Springer said. He took out his cell and snapped a picture. "So, we've got the chief's 'sunny banks.' What do you know."

"I figured we'd find banks of some kind," Reagan said. "When you aim toward the river, you can't go far without running up on some kind a' slough."

"Them's blackgum trees, Reagan, and that pond's

solid algae under those leaves."

"Can you imagine if somebody was to come riding through here on a horse or a motorcycle? They could run right into that bog. Never be heard of again."

Springer stopped, stiffened his back. "Reagan, would you stop that?"

"Stop what?"

"Never heard from again." His lips twisted into a smirk.

"Well, it happens. I'm telling you it does."

"Who'd it happen to lately?"

"Well, I don't know. But I heard tell of a man out walking in the woods, squirrel hunting. His dog got bit by a squirrel, right through the tongue. That dog lit out running, and the man lit out after him. The next day, his sons went looking for him. They found his gun on the edge of a bog, but they never found hide nor hair of the man or the dog."

"The bog just swallowed him up, him and the dog, nothing left." Springer rolled his eyes skyward.

"That's what was said."

"Well, I'm telling you, Reagan, that doesn't happen that way. Something is always left. Teeth, bones. Something will be left." He punctuated each word with a poke of his finger.

"If you say so, Sergeant."

"I say so, and if you don't believe me, ask the chief."

Reagan stopped suddenly. "Would you look at that." He took off his hat and waved it in front of his face.

"What *is* that?" Springer asked.

"It's a hovel. Vines near 'bout swallowed it up."

"Guess we need to check it out."

"I'm not going near it, Springer. Don't you know

what that is?"

Springer stretched out his lips and toggled his head. "No, Reagan, I don't know what it is, but I'm sure you do."

"That's Old Mose's cabin."

"And who in the name of God is Old Mose?"

"Some folks say he's a bear, some say he ain't. Whatever he is, he's a helluva mean cuss. He's killed cattle, people, but nobody's ever been able to bring him down. My daddy got off a shot at him once, but the dang thing, taller than you and me both, kept running."

"And this bear—or whatever—lives in a cabin, I suppose." Springer took another step toward the hovel.

"That's what they say, a little cabin all covered up with vines."

"Reagan, I swanny. You got some of the most harebrained ideas. Bears don't live in hovels."

"They can if they want to. Why not?"

"Why not, why not? Cause they're bears, that's why not." Springer stepped off the trail and approached the cabin.

Reagan held back, his hand hovered over his gun. "Springer, I wouldn't go in there if I was you."

Springer jerked his head back toward Reagan and held his finger to his lips.

Reagan slowly approached, hand still hovered over his gun.

Springer got to the door and tugged at it. It dragged against the ground. He leaned into the darkness, then pulled out his flash light and shot in a beam.

"What's in there?" Reagan asked.

"Come look for yourself, scaredy-cat."

Reagan crept forward until Springer had gone in. He

hastened his pace, and just as he reached the entrance, Springer yelled "boo," sending Reagan hotfooting it to the nearest tree.

Springer let out a belly laugh and doubled over, holding his sides.

"Very funny, very dang funny."

"Your face!" Springer said, still doubled over. "You looked like you'd seen the real Old Mose."

"What do you know about Old Mose?" Reagan eyed him suspiciously.

"There really was an Old Mose," Springer said, "but not around here, goofball. You know, the one in Colorado, a huge grizzly, killed a bunch 'a folks."

"Well, we got our Old Mose, too. And that there's his cabin." He sneezed, then pulled out his handkerchief and blew his nose.

"Right." Springer shook his head and snickered. "Old Mose, my eye."

"You smell that?"

Springer sniffed. "Smell what?"

"Smells like sulfur."

Springer sniffed again. "I don't smell anything."

He stepped in, sneezed again. "I swear I think it's coming from in here."

"Would you get out of there, Reagan?"

He poked his head out and motioned for Springer to come.

"Oh, all right, but I'm telling you there's nothing in there." Springer reached the door.

"Look at this." Reagan was kneeling on the dirt floor and tugging at a lock attached to a hinge. "It's a trap door."

"It sure does look like one. How'd I miss that?"

"How we gonna' get it open?" Reagan tugged again.

Springer beamed his flashlight toward the ground. "The hinge is rusty, but the lock looks new. I don't know. Maybe we oughtn't to fool with it. Let me get a picture."

Reagan got to his feet and stood back while Springer took a picture of the lock. "Hold the light on it a minute," Springer said. He handed the flashlight to Reagan and snapped another picture of the lock, then, of the interior of the hovel. "Let's get on back, see what the chief wants us to do about this. For all we know, we could be breaking and entering. I wonder who owns this place."

"Heck if I know. Don't look like nobody uses it for nothin'."

****

When Olivera got back to the police station, a little after twelve, he found Springer and Reagan perched near the door to his cubicle. "What's up, guys?" He slipped through the retinue, wanting a bit of privacy to organize his thoughts. Springer's red head soon popped in.

"We been waiting for you, Chief."

"I see that."

Springer entered, followed by Reagan.

"So, what'd you find?" Olivera said.

Springer held out a photograph. "Check this out, Chief."

"You found the 'sunny banks,' did you?"

"We sure did."

"This is what you call a gum brake, Lieutenant," Reagan added. "I don't know if you've got gum trees in California, but 'round here, when a bunch of blackgums congregate like that, we call 'em gum brakes."

Olivera nodded. "Very good, Reagan."

"Some don't call 'em blackgums. They call 'em

tupelos. It's an Indian name—means 'water tree.' "

"You sound like an expert."

"I looked that last part up on the web. You ever seen a gum tree before?"

"Don't know that I have."

"Yeah, they grow in marshy places along the river."

"Where'd you find this place?" Olivera said.

"Off the bridle path," Springer said. "You see that green stuff peeping through the leaves? That's algae. It looks like the ground, but it's not. It's water covered in green algae—common around here."

Olivera slipped Springer's photograph into his folder with the post-mortems of John Doe. "Did you find anything else?"

"Yeah, we did," Springer said. "A little cabin all covered in vines, not far from the gum brake."

"A cabin, eh?" Olivera said.

"More like a hovel. It was empty, but then Reagan happened to see a trap door on the floor."

"And?"

"We couldn't open it," Springer said. "Well, we could've shot the lock off, but then we got to thinking maybe that wasn't such a good idea—breaking and entering and all. We figured we might need a warrant."

"Good work, Springer," Olivera said. "That was the right choice, not to shoot the lock off. We *will* need a warrant, but I don't see any problem with that. I'll drop by the courthouse after lunch."

Springer and Reagan, apparently satisfied with themselves, returned to their desks in the outer office, leaving Olivera alone with his thoughts. He leaned back in his big executive, then sat up straight. "Hey, Springer."

"Yeah, Chief."

"Tell you what. Give Judge Hendricks's clerk a call. Ask her when the judge is going to be in today."

"Sure thing, Chief."

Olivera opened the folder and pulled out the photographs. Might be time to start an evidence board. "Hey, Springer, can you bring me one of those new evidence boards?"

"Sure, Chief, but I thought you preferred that computer thingamabob."

"I'm thinking we got some nice photos here, and I'd just soon be staring at them as gray walls."

Springer was back in a flash with a board and watched as Olivera hung it on the partition to the side of his desk. The board had a circle in the middle labeled "conclusion." Olivera stuck the John Doe pictures to the left of the circle and the "sunny banks" picture above it. "Not much to go on yet," Olivera said. "Will you get me those photographs you took of the house and garage? Not much to go on at all."

"Sure thing, Chief."

Olivera was hoping to hear from Eads soon, hoping for test results and DNA evidence. But what would be really nice was a couple of suspects. Yep. He didn't have a one, with the possible exception of Jack Eldridge. He leaned toward the door and called for Springer.

"Yeah, Chief."

"See if you can hunt up a photograph of Martin J. 'Jack' Eldridge and the building where his business is located—Eldridge and Son Barge Lines, Inc., Vicksburg, Mississippi."

"You stop at the Plantation Tea Room?"

"I didn't see it. You sure it's still there?"

"I thought for sure you'd pass it. It's right there where you cross the bridge."

"Well, it's not there anymore. Sorry. What's so special about pecan pralines?"

Springer half-closed his eyes and waggled his head as if he were drifting into a swoon. "Ga-lee, Chief, you haven't lived till you've eaten a pecan praline." He slumped away, limp-armed, shaking his head. "No pralines," Olivera heard him say to Reagan. Groans followed.

Olivera leaned toward the board, a thumb tack clinched between his teeth. "Victim," he mumbled. He stretched an elastic band from the circle to the photographs of John Doe and anchored it with a tack. "Sunny Banks garage," he mumbled, "death scene." He tacked the snapshot of the house and garage to the board. "Hey, Springer."

"Yeah, Chief." Springer came back in with his cellphone held to his chest. "Judge Hendricks is over there now, but he's leaving for lunch at one."

"Then I'd better get over there."

Springer held the phone to his lips. "He's coming now."

Olivera stood and grabbed his hat. "After I see the judge, I'll drop back by. We need to take a look at the cabin, and I want you and Reagan to come with me, so don't run off."

Chapter Fourteen

Police Station
November 4, 2:00 p.m.

Olivera checked his gun for bullets and slipped it into his holster. He felt his pockets for his tablet and pencil and his breast pocket for his shield. "Have you guys had lunch?"

"Yeah, Chief, we grabbed a baloney sandwich."

"You got gloves, evidence cards?"

"I got all that stuff, cones, too."

"Let's head out, then," Olivera said. "I want to take the jeep, in case we run into any rough patches in the woods."

"I'd better check the battery."

"The battery?"

"Chief, we haven't touched the jeep in weeks," Springer droned.

"Okay, okay, check the battery." Olivera turned back toward his cubicle. "Has the jeep got gas?"

"I'll check that, too." Springer jammed his arms into his jacket. "Let's go, Reagan. You got ever'thing? Your flashlight workin'?"

"Let me get some extra batteries." Reagan fished in his bottom drawer. "Go ahead. I'll be out in a second."

Springer, in the garage, lifted the hood to check the battery, then cranked the engine. It started right up. He rolled down the window, shouting to Reagan. "Get in, will you? I'd like to be back before dark."

Reagan piled in the back.

"I assume you know where you're going," Olivera said as he got into the passenger seat.

"Course I do. We just came back from there this morning."

"You aren't going to get us stuck in the mud, are you?"

Springer sighed and backed out of the garage.

Reagan leaned forward. "Springer, you bring the tool box?"

"It's back there, but whatcha need tools for? This is a simple operation." He pressed hard on the accelerator.

Reagan flopped back. "I'm just studying the situation." He buckled his seatbelt. "Maybe we oughta unscrew the hinges on the trap door. We wouldn't have to shoot off the lock. When we finish, we might wanna close it up nice and neat. Nobody'll know we've been there."

Olivera twisted around in his seat. "Smart thinking, Reagan."

"Thanks, Lieutenant. You see, my big brother had a hiding place, and me and my other brother slipped in there now and again. He had a padlock on the trap door, but we unscrewed the hinges. He never knew the differ'nce."

"Yeah, I bet he didn't," Springer said, unconvinced.

"Reagan," Olivera said, "I never took you for a sneak."

He snickered. "You know how it is between brothers…getting into one another's stuff."

"I wouldn't know," Olivera said. "I don't have a

brother."

"Must've been a lonely childhood, Chief," Springer said.

"No, I had lots of friends, cousins…tons of cousins."

Springer slapped his hand against the steering wheel and slowed down.

"What's the matter?" Olivera said.

"I just missed the dang turn off. Talking, not paying attention." Springer pulled off at the next road, backed up, and headed back onto Little Smith. A mile or so farther along, they came to Sunny Banks Cutoff. He turned right and followed the gravel road into the woods.

"How far till we get to the bridle path?" Olivera asked.

"About a quarter of a mile," Springer said.

"You think we can stick with the jeep?"

"We can make it down to the bog. Then we'd do well to walk. We got any wading boots back there?"

Reagan looked over the back seat. "Two pair's all."

"I guess one of us will be wading in his shoes," Springer said, "or staying in the jeep."

"It's not that wet, is it?" Olivera asked. "We haven't had any rain in a week."

"Boots'll do more than keep your feet dry, Chief."

Olivera squirmed uncomfortably.

They came to the bridle path and continued on till they got to the gum brake. "Whatcha think, Chief?"

"What a picture," Olivera exclaimed. He stepped out and sank in water. "Damn." He stepped back in the jeep. "You could have warned me." He frowned at Springer, who muffled a laugh. "You guys just can't grow up, can you?"

"Hand the chief a pair of hip boots, Reagan."

Olivera and Reagan in boots, Springer in his sock feet, pants rolled to his plump, white knees, slogged their way to the cabin. Olivera circled it and came back to the door. "Looks like the vines have taken over."

"They'll do that," Springer said.

Reagan entered the cabin first, followed by Springer and Olivera, and knelt next to the trap door.

"Go ahead and loosen the screws." Springer directed a beam toward the hinges. "We could open up a window. It's musty as hell in here."

"No," Olivera said, "let's not disturb anything we don't have to."

"I thought these screws might be corroded," Reagan said, "being out here in the damp and all, but they're not bad." He dropped the screws in his pocket and pulled up the door.

"My lord," Springer said, "it's dark down there." He held his flashlight to the side of his head and peered down. "There's a ladder going down, looks like about seven, eight feet."

"You first, Springer." Olivera slipped off his hip boots.

Springer squeezed his bulky hips through the opening and, stepping onto the first rung, made his way slowly down the ladder. "Piece of cake, Chief." He clicked on his flashlight.

"What's down there?" Olivera squatted next to the opening.

"Looks like a kid's hideout."

"Nothing but kid stuff?"

"No, there's some other stuff."

"Like what?" Olivera said. "And don't touch anything whatever you do."

101

"I won't." Springer stepped off the bottom rung onto the dirt floor.

"What else do you see?"

"An old desk, a computer case, zipped up."

"Well, don't unzip it, not yet. I'd better get down there," Olivera said to Reagan. "Give me a hand, and get your boots off."

Holding onto Reagan's arm, Olivera climbed down. "This *is* a hideout, a kid's hideout. So what are we doing down here?"

"Look closer, Chief." Springer flashed a beam across the walls, illuminating shelves stacked with bottles and jars, from the ceiling to the floor.

"What on earth?" Olivera slipped on latex gloves.

"Looks to me like a bootlegger's been operating out of here. White lightning."

"Bootlegger?" Olivera grimaced. "Arkansas's been wet since—when did it go wet?"

"In 1933," Springer said, "but only half the state went wet—thirty-seven dry counties, thirty-eight wet."

"More to the point, when did Dent County go wet?"

"The year Reagan was born," Springer said, "1942."

"I heard that," Reagan said. "I ain't that old."

Springer laughed.

Reagan beamed his light into the hole. "What's down there, Springer?"

"A lot of old liquor bottles." He lifted a bottle and held it to his nose. "Reckon we oughta take one of these in?"

"What's it smell like?" Olivera asked.

"Hard to say. If I remember rightly, white lightning don't have much of a smell. You know, it don't matter, Dent County being wet, Chief. A bootlegger could make a killing selling to underage kids, and Hembree's got a peck of 'em."

"You mean at the college?" Olivera said.

"Maybe the Eldridge boy was running an operation," Springer said. "A kid could come riding back here, pick up his hooch, light out, nobody'd be the wiser."

"We'd better take a couple of these." Olivera handed a bottle to Springer. "We can fingerprint them back at the lab."

"What about the computer, Chief?"

"Yeah, we'll take that, too. Any of these bottles have anything in them?"

Springer ran his light over the bottles, shelf by shelf, till he came to one with a good inch of clear liquid in the bottom. "That one does."

"Let's take it. Bag it."

In the middle of the room, stood an old-fashioned desk with a hole for an inkwell. "I haven't seen one of these in a while." Olivera pointed at the top of the desk. "Look at this, Springer. A desk calendar. 'Eldridge and Son Barge Lines, Inc.,' and an ash tray with a towboat on it." He picked it up. " 'The Rhonda Sue.' "

Springer focused his beam on the desk. "Must've been the Eldridge kid's hideout."

"It's on Eldridge property." Reagan leaned over the hole.

"Yeah, but that don't mean nothing," Springer said. "People don't have much respect for property rights along the river. Anybody could have used this place. That's probably why they kept this room locked."

"Makes sense," Olivera said. "There's a number written on the calendar. Get a picture of that, Springer."

"That's a Mississippi area code, Chief."

"Let's check it out. Might lead to something."

"Want me to call it?"

"No, we'll look it up when we get back to the station." Olivera bent down and looked inside the compartment under the top of the desk, then slipped his hand in. "What have we here?" He brought out a box of bullets. "Huh, forty-five caliber. Bag these for me." He looked again and pulled out a bottle. "A bottle of bore solvent. Whoever he is, he keeps his piece clean." He handed Springer the bottle. "A cleaning rod, cleaning patches, and gun oil."

"I guess you want all this bagged, too," Springer said.

"Yeah, anything that could hold a print." Olivera passed his beam over the floor, then the ceiling. "Quite a collection of pennants: Arkansas Razorbacks, Blanchard College…Hembree Boll Weevils? Ha."

"Don't you go knocking our mascot, Lieutenant," Reagan called down.

Olivera snickered. He ran his light from the ceiling to the floor. "Would you look at that, an old croquet set."

"You want that bagged, Chief?" Springer said.

"Let's pass on that for the time being. I can't imagine there'd be any fresh prints on it."

"Unless the assailant conked John Doe across the back of the head with a croquet mallet," Reagan said.

Olivera looked up through the hole. "Reagan, you surprise me."

"Why's that, Lieutenant?"

"Your acumen for tomfoolery."

"Could you put that in plain English?"

"Insight, Reagan. Insight."

Olivera finished his scrutiny of all the surfaces. "Okay, guys, let's get going. I think we've seen enough for today. You need help with that, Springer?"

"I got it. You go ahead," Springer said, then added, "Chief, did you see these trophies?"

"Yeah, what about them?"

"This one's got a name on it. 'Martin J. "Johnny" Eldridge III. First in Polo. Hembree Country Club.' "

Chapter Fifteen

Yacht Club, Hembree
November 4, 8:00 p.m.

The Hembree Marina was one of a few places
between Memphis and New Orleans to offer fuel and
deep water dockage to river travelers. On Wednesday
nights, locals and out-of-towners hazarded the swaying
footbridge to the Marina's Yacht Club to feast on shrimp,
crab, and oysters, shipped in daily from the Gulf Coast.

Around eight that evening, Mosey and Nadia lined
up at the buffet while Robert and Hugh waited for a table.

"Lauren left, I'm assuming." Nadia picked up plates
for herself and Mosey.

"Yeah," Mosey said, "she wanted to get back to
Philadelphia before the bad weather hit, but between me
and you—" She glanced at Robert and Hugh. "—I'm not
sure that was it at all." She reached for a crab leg. "You
want one of these?"

Nadia shook her head. "What was it if not the
weather?"

"The *body*, of course."

"Wouldn't run me off," Nadia said, "not if I liked
the place."

Standing before a platter of fried butterfly shrimp,
Mosey spooned a helping onto her plate and another onto
Nadia's. "I've always wondered why it was called Sunny

Banks—haven't you?"

"The gum brake and the slough—must be," Nadia said.

"Maybe," Mosey said. "Not sure how long it's been called that. Could be when the house was first built, the family had a dock or maybe a houseboat on the river." She picked up a stuffed crab. "You want one of these?"

"I'll pass." Nadia looked sideways at Mosey. "You think they'd allow a private dock right on the river?"

"Yum, fried okra." Mosey scooped up a serving. "Does seem a little treacherous."

Nadia plucked a piece from Mosey's plate.

"Hey!"

"Just checking to see if it's good and crispy." Nadia held out her plate, and Mosey scooped up another serving.

"The current is pretty strong, even along the banks," Mosey said. "Remember that fool guy—what was his name?—who tried to swim across on graduation night?"

"A professional swimmer couldn't swim that river, much less a drunk teenager."

"What are you ladies jabbering about?" Hugh asked.

Mosey frowned. "Jabbering, huh."

Nadia snickered. "What are you guys *jabbering* about?"

"Nothing important," Hugh said.

"I thought I heard Lauren Wilson's name mentioned." Mosey winked at Nadia.

"Yeah," Robert said, "I drove her back to Little Rock this morning."

"Did she say anything?" Mosey skewered an ear of corn.

"What do you mean *anything*?"

"About buying a house, silly?"

Robert sneaked a hushpuppy off Mosey's plate.

"Would y'all keep your cotton-pickin' fingers out of my plate?"

"There," Robert said. "I'll trade you a frog leg."

"I don't *want* a frog leg." She tossed it back.

"She didn't have much to say about that," Robert said.

"About what?" Nadia asked.

"About buying a house."

"Did she say anything at all?" Mosey said.

"She said she liked the places she'd seen." Robert finished filling his plate and, picking up napkins for the four of them, led the way to the table.

"She didn't mention Sunny Banks?" Mosey said.

"She asked me if I'd heard any more about the incident." He pulled a chair out for Mosey.

"You mean the body?" Mosey said, sitting.

"I told her what I'd read in the paper, which she already knew." Robert waved to a server. "Could we get some drinks, please?"

"Certainly." The server set a basket of buttery Texas toast in the middle of the table and pulled out his order pad and ballpoint. "What can I get for you?"

"Margaritas for Mosey and me."

The server nodded to Nadia. "And you, ma'am?"

"A mojito, extra lime."

"And you, sir?"

"Bring me an Imperial IPA," Hugh said, "in a cold mug."

The server hurried away, dodging in-coming customers on his way to the bar.

"As I was saying," Mosey continued, dropping her

napkin in her lap, "at happy hour, she seemed sort of—"

"What?" Robert took a slice of toast and passed the basket to Nadia.

"I don't know, sort of distracted." Mosey shrugged. "She didn't have much to say, which I thought was weird."

"Maybe she's shy." Nadia split her toast and put back half.

"Seems like she'd be eager to find out more about Hembree," Mosey said. "If I had two months to remodel a house, you'd better believe I'd be asking questions."

"But she hasn't decided on a house," Nadia said.

"I know. That body quashed it."

"What do you mean *quashed it*?" Hugh took a piece of toast and held the basket for Mosey.

"She's exaggerating," Nadia said to Hugh.

"You were not there, missy." Mosey frowned at Nadia and took the half piece.

"I didn't have to be." Nadia smirked.

"Okay, whatever. But I'm telling you—" Mosey glanced at Hugh. "—if Lauren changes her mind, I wouldn't be surprised in the least."

The server arrived with a tray of frosty drinks and distributed them among the foursome.

Hugh took a sip of his beer. "A job in academia is nothing to sneeze at."

"Well, I know that. I live with an academic, don't I?"

Nadia paused to think. "I see what you mean. It is a tad off-putting."

"More than a tad," Mosey said.

"Ladies, please." Hugh moaned, inserting a fork tine into the tip of a crab leg. "She's a forensic psychologist.

Doubtful a body would cause her to renege, not on the offer we made."

Robert, teeth sunk in an ear of corn, gave a nod.

"That good, eh?" Nadia poked a spoon of étouffée in Mosey's direction. "Try this. It's *so* tasty."

"As good as it gets at the assistant professor level," Hugh said. "A hefty salary, a reduced teaching load, and a hundred thousand in start-up money for a lab."

"Wow, her colleagues are going to hate her," Mosey said. "So what would it take to make her turn all that down?"

"It'd have to be something huge, I would think." Hugh jiggled out a piece of crab meat and popped it in his mouth.

"Yeah," Mosey said, "*really* huge."

"Huge like…?" Nadia asked.

"Like maybe she knew something about that body," Mosey said.

Robert's posture wilted as he opened and closed his mouth. "Whatever you are imagining about our soon-to-be colleague—" He glared at Mosey. "—keep it to yourself, *please*."

"Yes," Hugh said, "probably not a good idea to start a rumor."

"I have no intention of starting a rumor," Mosey said, "but I had a bad feeling about all this at happy hour. Her behavior was not normal. She was *very* distracted, kept pulling her phone out of her purse and sticking it back. She must have done that a dozen times. And it surprises me that you two, being behavioral scientists yourselves, didn't notice."

"Oh, I noticed." Hugh wiped his chin. "She was definitely distracted, sort of lost her spark, actually, but

I figured she was put off by the...well, not exactly the body. It was more like she was worried she wasn't going to get the house."

"And that's another thing," Mosey said. "Why such an interest in Sunny Banks? It's not even on the market. I only knew about it because John Earle told me."

"She's got a point," Nadia said. "How did she know?"

Hugh looked at Mosey. "Why didn't you ask her?"

"I did, and she said it was on the Hembree site. But then she tacked on something about meeting some guy when she was here before. Met him at the Tavernette bar. Said he was telling her about the better neighborhoods. It didn't seem important at the time, but now I wish I'd found out more. And you know something else? That property is a lot bigger than I thought it was—the land, I mean. There's a good bit of acreage between the house and the river. I wonder if she's interested in that, too, or just the lot the house is on."

"Sounds like a good excuse to phone her," Nadia said.

"Seems like a moot point," Mosey said.

"Moot point?" Hugh reached for his mug.

"Doubtful it'll go on the market. They'll have to wait for Olivera to release it."

"How long will that take?" Robert said.

"Depends. If they clear up this business with the body, it could list in a few weeks, but I don't see that happening. They don't even have an ID on the victim."

"They're not sure it was a homicide," Nadia said. "He could've died from a fall."

"If you ignore the fact he was found in the front seat of a car, maybe you could think he died from a fall."

Mosey rolled her eyes.

"If you're thinking Lauren could be a suspect," Robert said, "we're more likely suspects than she. We were here at least. She was in Philadelphia." He sipped his margarita to the bottom and set the glass aside.

"Who said anything about her being a suspect?" Mosey stared at Robert. "I just think a couple of pieces of circumstantial evidence need to be cleared up, that's all."

"You're not thinking of calling Olivera, are you?" Nadia said to Mosey.

"Of course, not. I have no intention of ratting out my client. But if Olivera should contact me, say, ask me directly, I'd feel obligated to air my suspicions."

Robert heaved a loud sigh and stood. "I need another drink."

Chapter Sixteen

Thursday, November 5, 8:30 a.m.
Morgue, Delta Infirmary

Mosey wasn't the only one feeling the need to air suspicions. Gus Olivera hurried through his morning routine, made a brief stop at the station, then got back in his car and headed to Delta Infirmary.

He tapped quietly before entering the morgue, then opened the door a crack. McGinnis was in her usual place. "Morning, Doc."

"Good morning, Lieutenant. You're up with the chickens."

He glanced at the clock on the white tile wall above the autopsy table. "It's not so early. Did you get the evidence from the cabin?"

"It's right there." She gestured toward the stainless steel counter. "What are we calling that place?"

"OMC." He laughed. "Kids around here used to call it 'Old Mose's cabin.' "

"Who is Old Mose?"

"You don't know?" He grinned. "You're from around here."

"Before my time, I guess."

"I don't know if there ever was an Old Mose," he said, "but his cabin is still here. It's down by the river on the property behind Sunny Banks."

"Part of the Eldridge place?"

He nodded. "I sent Springer and Reagan to see if they could figure out why it's called that." He pulled a photograph out of his breast pocket. "Springer snapped this yesterday."

"Wow. Looks like a gum brake."

"It is, and the cabin's close by. Prettiest little place. A small brick building, about six by six, with a wooden door. The whole thing's covered in ivy except the door. They checked it out yesterday morning. Found a trap door on the dirt floor. Seemed like it was worth looking into, so I got a warrant, and we ran over there yesterday afternoon."

"Find anything important?"

"What you've got here." He slipped the photograph in his pocket and glanced at the items Springer had bagged. "Some old liquor bottles. One had something in it. Springer thinks it might be pure grain alcohol, white lightning, he called it."

"And all that gun paraphernalia," she said. "From bullets to gun oil, but no gun."

"That's right. But I'd be interested to know if there's a gun registered to Martin J. Eldridge III."

"You think this is his stuff?"

"Could be. There was an old desk, like an old-fashioned school desk. The gun paraphernalia was inside the compartment under the top, and there was a desk calendar from Eldridge and Son Barge Lines, and an ashtray with a picture of a towboat, the Rhonda Sue."

"Hmm. Rhonda Sue Eldridge, must be…Martin Sr.'s daughter."

"Did you know her?"

"*Of* her. Like I said, our families weren't that

friendly."

"Right."

"So, that was it—bottles and gun paraphernalia?"

"There was a phone number on the desk calendar. Could lead to something. And a polo trophy with Johnny Eldridge's name on it. But the big thing was the lap top. It's still at the station. Might learn something from that if we can get into the files."

"That shouldn't be a problem."

"I know you haven't had a chance to examine the new evidence, but I thought I'd drop by, talk to you about my trip to Vicksburg…if you can spare the time."

"Sure." She covered the corpse and slipped off her gloves. "Did you take the river road?"

"I did. Very nice."

"Did you find out anything?" Eads took a seat at her desk, and Olivera propped himself on the edge.

"Yes and no. I talked to Jack Eldridge. He seemed like a nice enough guy. I was expecting something different. He agreed to see me right away, stopped whatever he was doing, answered all my questions. The man had *innocent* written all over him, his expression, his body language—"

"And yet?"

He nodded. "I had a feeling he knew something."

"Like?"

"I don't know." He shrugged. "Maybe he's aware of something. Something he's not involved in. That river bunch is a close community. It's highly unlikely he'd blow the whistle even if he *did* know something."

"Especially if that *something* involved family. He didn't recognize John Doe, I'm assuming."

"No, but he offered to send the picture to the boat

captains. It's a long shot, but as we were saying the other day, right now the only thing we've got is Sunny Banks. We can't connect the victim with anyone except the Eldridges, and that's tenuous. We don't have a clue as to who he was, where he lived, what he did, or why he was there." Olivera stood up and began to pace. "You think we can hurry up the DNA?"

"I can try—" She heaved a deep sigh. "—but there's no guarantee that's going to lead to an identification. And I'm sorry to say I haven't heard anything back from medical records, which makes me wonder if he isn't from out of state."

"Yeah, doesn't look like John Doe is a local man. I've shown the post-mortem photographs to half a dozen Hembreeites, and nobody recognizes him. Shepherd did say he looked vaguely familiar. If he lived here, he must have been a newcomer, not part of the old set."

"You could show it to Ruby at the Tavernette. If he's been here any time at all, she'd recognize him."

"Hey—" He smiled and nodded. "—that's a good idea. I think I'll run by there on my way back to the station."

"By the way," she said, "I've been going over the wound again. More bruising has shown up, and I'm inclined to think this was an assault. The bruising around the gash has a particular shape to it."

"Not like the end of a croquet mallet, is it?"

"Croquet mallet? What made you think of that?"

"Oh, something Reagan said. There was a croquet set at the cabin."

She furrowed her brow. "If the assailant had used a croquet mallet, you would expect a rounded, smallish bruise. This is more narrow, longer."

"Like what?"

She picked up a piece of paper and drew. "About this shape."

"Hmm." Olivera rubbed his chin. "The blade of a hockey stick has a similar shape."

"But if you hit someone with a hockey stick, the area of contact would correspond to the toe, would it not?"

"Maybe," he said, "or the heel." He whacked at the air with an imaginary stick. "Yeah, not a hockey stick, but what? What *did* he use?" Baffled, he paced toward the autopsy table and then away from it, stopping periodically to shake his head. He looked at McGinnis, still at her desk, thumping her desk pad with the eraser end of a pencil. "It's as if we were at a play." He paused in front of her desk. "The stage is empty except for a prop here, a prop there."

She looked up, then around the room, as if she were trying to picture his scenario.

"We see the props—" He walked away from her. "—but we don't know *why* they are there, how they're connected, or what they have to do with the dead man...slumped over the steering wheel of a car." He came to a halt, then turned toward the autopsy table. "We can see the place, and we know the time, but the actors are missing. And, come to think of it, we don't even have a crime scene." He threw up his hands. "A death scene, yes, but no crime scene."

"So, I guess we're stuck for the time being." She picked up her pencil and resumed her thumping. "At least till we get an ID on the victim."

"You'll let me know," he said, "if you hear anything?"

"Of course."

"And rush the DNA, if you can. Meanwhile, I think I'll follow up on Ruby." He tipped his hat to McGinnis and, leaving the morgue, pulled out his cellphone. "Springer," he said, heading down the wide hall to the exit, "glad I caught you."

"What's up, Chief?"

"I need you to do me a favor."

"Sure, Chief."

"Grab the post-mortem photographs of the victim. They're in the folder on my desk. You'll see them. Meet me at the Tavernette, say, in ten minutes. By the way, is Reagan around?"

"Yeah, he is."

"Is he busy?"

"Not really."

"Bring him with you. I'll treat you guys to a cup of coffee."

Chapter Seventeen

November 5, 9 a.m.
Frye, Frye, and Humphrey

Mosey hesitated outside the door to her father's old law firm. It seemed a little early to pop in unannounced, though Dot always told her to come by anytime. "Dot," she said, finally sticking her head in.

Dot emerged from the kitchenette. "Mosey! Come in, come in. If you've come to see Carlotta, you're a little early, but she should be here soon."

"Is that fresh coffee I smell?" Mosey asked.

"Sure is. You want a cup?"

"I'd love one," she said as she slumped onto the leather sofa.

"You okay?" Dot dropped the towel she was using to dry her hands on the end table and sat next to Mosey.

"Dot, I'm not as young as I used to be. We went to the Yacht Club last night, and the second margarita didn't dock so well."

"They make them way too strong, if you ask me. I tell them to water mine down."

"I didn't know you were a margarita fan." The thought of it brightened up her sour frame of mind.

"I've been known to drink one on occasion," Dot said with a wink. "Let me get your coffee."

Mosey relaxed onto a leather throw pillow, her eyes

drifting around the room. The cool darkness of the bookcases and heavy furniture, the smell of leather and wood made her nostalgic for her childhood. She'd spent a month of Sundays there waiting to see her daddy. Hardly a thing had changed, even with the advent of her step-aunt Carlotta's tenure as Chief Executive Officer. Carlotta had chosen to leave things just as they were. A smart move on her part. The clients of Frye, Frye, and Humphrey weren't fans of change. The same tall mahogany shelves lined the wall across from the entrance, and her granddaddy Amos's portrait still dominated the wall behind Dot's desk. It was just like him to linger there, looking over Dot's shoulder. The leather sofa was in the same spot, as were the upholstered arm chairs. It was all the same. The only thing missing was…

A tad nostalgic, are we?

She didn't answer, just smiled.

You know you could speak to Carlotta about what's bothering you.

She lowered her brow. "Daddy, you been reading my mind?"

Before he could answer, Dot pattered in with the coffee, cream, and sugar. "Here we go, just like you like it. Nice and hot, and there's some fresh half-and-half. I picked it up at the market this morning."

"Thanks so much." Mosey sat up, spooned in sugar, then added a big glug of half-and-half.

"So you were at the Yacht Club, you say?"

"Yeah, Robert, Nadia, Hugh, and I."

"Oh, I like that young man Hugh. You think he and Nadia are interested?"

"Romantically, you mean?"

Dot nodded.

"I don't know. Sometimes I think so, but neither seems to be pushing it."

"When I was a girl, men and women weren't just friends. They were either an item, as you young ones say, or they were, well, nothing."

"I know. Momma used to say that. She didn't quite get friendships between men and women."

"Now your Aunt Carlotta—" Dot sat in one of the upholstered chairs. "—she likes men. She has lots of men friends."

The door opened and Carlotta stepped in. "My ears are burning. You guys wouldn't be talking about me, would you?"

Dot's mouth flew open. "Course not, Carlotta." She stood.

"Aunt Carlotta." Mosey stood, too. "How are you?" She gave her a hug. "I was hoping I might catch you in."

"You're here early, girl. What's up?"

"Well, I wanted to talk to you about a little business matter, if you've got the time."

"Always for you, sweetie. Come on in."

From the reception Carlotta had given her, you'd think she and Mosey were thick as thieves, but that was not the case. For reasons neither fathomed, they had never become close, though they ought to have been. Carlotta had lost her father, then her mother not long after her mother had married Amos Frye. And Mosey, whose mother died when she was a child, had lost her grandfather a couple of years after his second wife died. Her father then passed away some few years later. Two orphans, you'd think, would have clung to each other like shipwrecked sailors to a plank. But they had not.

Each had her own life to lead, Carlotta as head of the family firm and Mosey as a new bride. Mosey regretted Carlotta's reticence to act like a real aunt but, at the same time, recognized she hadn't done all she could have to welcome Carlotta into the family.

Carlotta, with Mosey at her side, entered her office and dropped her briefcase next to her chair. "So, tell me—" She turned to offer Mosey a seat. "—what business matter are we talking about?"

"Sunny Banks." Mosey sat in the chair nearest Carlotta's desk and looked around the room. "You haven't changed a thing in here. It's just like Daddy left it, except for his old desk, which I'm really enjoying. Thanks for letting me take it. Technically, it should have stayed with the firm."

"I know, but who cares? I know your daddy would have wanted you to have it if he'd known you liked it." She smiled and sat next to Mosey. "Hold on a minute, would you?" She got up, walked to the door, and spoke to Dot, then returned to her seat. "We should be good for half an hour."

"I know your time's valuable. This shouldn't take long. I just wanted to ask you about the Eldridge property. John Earle told me this morning he'd spoken with you."

"I thought Jack was going to list it right away. We were getting the necessary papers in order, but now, with this body showing up in Martin's car, I guess it's a no-go, till Olivera solves the crime—if there was a crime."

"I guess I should tell Lauren Wilson—she's the potential buyer—that it won't be listed for the time being."

"That's my understanding," Carlotta said. "I haven't

spoken with Jack, but that's the way these things usually play out. Property involved in a crime can't be claimed, sold, whatever, until the police release the evidence."

"But you know in this case," Mosey added, "the house might not have had anything to do with it."

Carlotta looked doubtful. "I don't know, Mosey. That'd be nice if the house were free and clear, but I'm not sure that it is."

"You're not sure?"

"Between you and me," she said, "this *incident*, as Olivera is calling it, has a bad smell to it. I don't think it's a coincidence the victim died or, more likely, was killed on the Eldridge property, then stuffed in the front seat of Martin's luxury automobile."

"You think it wasn't just a coincidence it occurred the way it did? You think the Eldridges were somehow involved?"

"You've been around lawyers all your life, Mosey, but maybe, because you were young, you were spared the blood and guts. When your client list is predominantly criminals—and I don't mean just the ones that sell drugs or conk folks over the head, I mean the ones in suits, too—well, you become suspicious. You start to look around corners, see things coming before they get there. What I'm seeing here is that it was no coincidence that somebody put a body to bleed out in the driver's seat of Old Man Eldridge's car. It smells like retribution to me, and more than that. What would I call it?—*mutiny*. Ha, that's a good word for it, the Eldridges being who they are." Carlotta stood and walked to the door, then turned back to Mosey. "You want a refill, hon?"

"No, thanks, I'm good." She set her cup on the table.

Carlotta spoke to Dot, then returned to the same spot, sat, and ran her fingers through her long, dark hair. "You were probably too young to remember this," she continued, "but wealth in Hembree at one time was divided between the planters and the river folks. The Eldridges were the oldest and biggest of the river magnates. Then, in the eighties, river traffic slowed way down, and the families with a business worth moving took it downriver to Vicksburg. I'm from there, and, though they aren't blood kin, mind you, my father's brother Maxwell Humphrey married an Eldridge, Rhonda Sue, Jack Eldridge's sister."

"I had no idea."

"Why would you?" Carlotta said with a shrug. "The Eldridges moved away from here maybe before you were born."

"But I thought they lived at Sunny Banks."

"They held on to the house, but they moved to Vicksburg. Then, when old Martin and his wife retired and turned the business over to Jack, they moved back to Sunny Banks. Jack rarely sets foot in Hembree except to visit his parents or stop by here occasionally. I doubt the old couple wanted the house sold, but Jack didn't want it to sit there empty. The insurance would have cost a fortune, not that money is that big a deal."

"But what's this about retribution, mutiny?"

"I don't know. That's just where my thoughts are going. Think about it. Why put a dead body in the driver's seat?"

"Well, I guess that could be symbolic, like some sort of slam against the boss man."

"And all that blood," Carlotta said. "I'm not sure *what* it means but it might mean something."

"Like blood revenge?" Mosey asked. "Yeah." She nodded, "I guess that's still a thing. Like the mafia always blowing each other away. It's sort of a family thing."

"*Honor* they call it," Carlotta said. "A family has to protect its honor, which could mean killing someone in the family or a member of another family."

"So this was some sort of feud?" Mosey said.

"It could be a feud, though I can't think of any feuds the Eldridges were involved in. Jack doesn't mess around. He's a straight shooter, keeps his business transactions on the up and up."

"Are there any other people involved in the business?"

"He's got a son, Johnny…Martin John Eldridge III."

"What's he like?" Mosey leaned in.

"I don't really know Johnny," Carlotta said, "but I can't say I have a great desire to know him."

"That sounds ominous."

Dot tapped lightly on the door and came in with Carlotta's coffee. She set it on the mahogany table, and checking her watch, said, "Carlotta, I don't want to rush you girls, but you've got an appointment, don't forget."

"Speaking of which," Carlotta said, "if you'd be a dear and get those files for me, I'll give them a quick once over before he gets here. Thanks, Dot." She sipped her coffee and, turning back to Mosey, said, "Now, where were we?"

"You were talking about Johnny Eldridge."

"Right, yeah, he's probably all right, but you know sometimes how a little thing can leave a bad impression?"

Mosey nodded.

"I was at a family gathering once, a big wedding, the whole bunch was there—all the Eldridges and Humphreys, mainly—and Johnny had had too much to drink. His daddy grabbed him by the shoulders and tried to walk him out of the reception, and Johnny hauled off and took a swing at him, cursed him for everything he was worth."

"Gosh, that's pretty awful."

"Yeah, it was. I don't think I've laid eyes on Johnny since, but like I say, I don't think I care to. His father is a decent man. But that son of his, I don't know, maybe he's just a spoiled brat. A little too big for his britches."

As Carlotta was ending her commentary on the younger Eldridge, Dot came back in with a short stack of files. "Here you go, Carlotta. Anything else you need?"

"No, I'll just take a quick look." She slipped on her readers. "Mosey, sorry I can't chat longer, but I'd better get ready for this appointment." She stood, and Mosey followed suit.

"That's okay. That was helpful what you told me. I'll run along. I need to get to the office anyway." Mosey followed Dot out. "Thanks, Dot." She set her empty cup down on the end table and headed out the door.

How'd it go?

The voice came just as Mosey got to the bottom of the stairs. The Square was fairly empty on a cool November morning. She looked around, didn't see anyone she knew. "Daddy, you were right."

About what?

"Talking to Carlotta."

What'd she tell you?

"She didn't exactly tell me anything. But in a vague sort of way, she pointed me in the right direction."

Mosey, that's about as clear as mud.

"Before long, it may be clearer than folks *want* it to be. You just wait."

Chapter Eighteen

November 5, 9:25 a.m.
Frye, Frye, and Humphrey

Dot stepped to Carlotta's door. "Your nine-thirty appointment called to reschedule. His wife's got the flu."

"Well, good grief. I could have had more time with Mosey." Carlotta picked up the stack of files and handed them back to Dot. "Did Mr. Randall reschedule?"

"He's coming in next week."

Carlotta sat in her desk chair and checked her watch. She had a good hour to burn. "Dot," she called, "would you bring me the Eldridge files, please, ma'am?"

"All of them?"

"All of them. Put them on a cart for me, would you?"

Carlotta's curiosity had started to gnaw. Two people that week had asked about the Eldridges. First, Gus Olivera. Now, Mosey. The Eldridges were among the firm's VIP clients, but she'd never had an occasion to dig into their history. Nothing of particular interest had arisen on her watch—a couple of matters related to Mr. Eldridge's estate, but no disputes, nothing complicated. What was in that thick file of theirs? It was worth a flip through, and now seemed as good a time as any. She got up and walked to the door.

Dot was at the file cabinet, leaning over an open drawer. "You know what, Carlotta? Some of these files are so old, they're coming apart at the seams. Look at that." She held up a classic red rope cachet portfolio. "They go back to the time of Edwin G. Siebels."

"Who?"

"Siebels, the inventor of the vertical filing system. You never heard of him?"

"When was that?"

"I think it was 1898…long before our time."

"Dot, you are a wealth of information."

"Oh, well, I did pick up a few totally worthless facts in secretarial school."

Carlotta smiled.

"There it all is." Dot heaved a sigh and rolled the cart into Carlotta's office. "Where you want this?"

"There by the table is good."

"You want a refill on that cup?"

"Not yet, I've barely touched it."

Dot left, and Carlotta moved back to the mahogany table. She wriggled out of her heels and picked up a stack of folders. Although tempted to start with the oldest— old law transactions being a fascination of hers—she postponed that treat and flipped through the more recent files. Forms—little else—peeked over the tops. She paused at a file that was color-coded in green and dated 1990. A thick folder was stuffed toward the middle. "Hmm…looks important." She pulled it out and flopped it on the table. As she opened the top folder, an old newspaper article slipped out. " 'Crew Missing in Towboat Accident,' " she read aloud. Another clipping, stappled to the article, read, "Captain of Towboat Refuses to Testify at Hearing." She stepped to the door. "Dot, you know anything about this?" She held up the article.

"What's that?"

"Looks like the Eldridges were involved in a lawsuit having to do with a towboat disaster in 1990."

"Uh-huh," she said. "I remember that. It was Ellis's case. Lasted a good long while. Seems like it ended up in the court in New Orleans."

"Says here, 'The captain of the *Billy Harding*, involved in last month's tugboat crash, has refused to testify at a hearing investigating the disaster.' "

"Who was the captain?" Dot asked. "It must say there somewhere."

" 'In addition to Captain Chester Bell,' " Carlotta read, " 'two company officials have also refused to address the hearing.' " She scanned the article, then continued reading. " 'The *Billy Harding* collided with a tanker carrying 10,000 gallons of sulfuric acid. One barge split in half, spilling large amounts of toxic cargo into the Mississippi River. Bell's role in the accident is pertinent to the resolution of the case brought by the families of two missing crew members believed to have drowned in the accident.' " She paused and looked at Dot. " 'The Coast Guard and law enforcement agencies from nearby towns, despite intensive efforts, were unable to rescue the missing men. Neither body has been recovered.' "

"Does it give the names of the victims?"

She scanned the article. "Here it is. 'Lionel M. Sanders of Hembree, Arkansas, and W. E. Jenkins of Vicksburg, Mississippi.' "

"Yes, that was a bad one," Dot said. "Can't remember exactly how that was resolved."

Carlotta looked at Dot askance, then returned to her office. She continued her scrutiny of the files till eleven o'clock, when her appointment arrived.

****

Later that day at the usual closing time, she stayed on and dove right back into the Eldridge files. She had a feeling there was something there and Dot, she was pretty sure, knew what it was—how could she not? But Dot wasn't telling, and that made Carlotta all the more eager to find it.

"Carlotta, I'm leaving now," Dot said. "Anything I can get you before I go?"

"No, I'm fine. I'm going to hang out here a little while, see if I can close this up."

"Don't stay too late. You've got an eight-thirty appointment tomorrow."

"I won't. You go on home. I'll be fine."

As Carlotta was saying good-bye to Dot, her eyes were already fixed on the next thick file. The label said, "Family Lines," which seemed a little unspecific. What *about* the Family Lines? Nearly everything she'd come across was about the towboat business. She opened an old portable file, green with a brown ribbon tied in a bow. As she untied the ribbon, she wondered whose fingers had last touched that bundle. Before making the bow, they'd tied a knot, a defensive gesture, she imagined, as if to place an obstacle in the path of the next person to *open* what had been *closed*. She herself had occasionally wondered who, at some future date, might retrieve the very file she had put away *once and for all*. Ellis had given her advice about that—"Carlotta, around these parts," he'd told her, "in Hembree especially more than the bigger towns, we deal with the same families, the same conflicts, over and again. If not land, water, or if not that, the wills of long-time settlers. The heirs of big estates rarely see eye to eye. So, Carlotta, do everything by the book 'cause you never know when some issue you've buried might pop up and grab somebody. Don't let that *somebody* be you, ya hear?"

Dot, a filing expert, had done everything according to Ellis's philosophy. Files didn't go missing on her guard, nothing was out of place. She was the true sentinel of the archive, the sphinx that Gus Olivera had mistakenly taken *her* for. "Family Lines, eh?" Carlotta mumbled. "What have we here?" She had no idea, but Dot knew. She'd place money on it.

She laid the folder on the table, sat, and rubbed the back of her neck. But before she resumed her scrutiny, she walked barefooted to the cabinet behind her desk, retrieved a crystal decanter, and poured two fingers of single-malt into a tumbler. Settling back into her chair, she took a sip and opened the file. "Family Lines, eh?" she repeated. She shuffled through the documents. "Huh," she mumbled. The usual letterheads, depositions, reports weren't there. The first sheet was labeled at the top, "Personal—Eldridge." Clipped to the document, which was blank except for the label, there was a carbon copy of a letter addressed to Hamilton Waite.

"Dear Mr. Waite," it began. "Pursuant to the matter we discussed in your office, my client is prepared to pay monthly expenses in the amount agreed upon (three hundred fifty dollars), deemed sufficient to cover your daughter's board, lodging, and medical expenses. A check in the aforementioned amount will be sent on the first of each month to the address you have provided (Miss Mona Waite, 426 S. Mariposa Dr., San Diego, California)." The letter was dated September 30, 1970 and signed, "Sincerely yours, Amos Frye, Attorney at

Law."

"That's strange." Had the letter been misfiled, accidentally mixed in with the "Family Lines" documents? She fumbled through the remainder of the file but found only blank sheets of typing paper and old legal pads. "How very odd." She'd never before seen such a file. She re-read the letter in which her step-father, Amos Frye, had agreed to send checks on somebody's behalf—one of the Eldridges, she assumed—to Mona Waite, Hamilton Waite's daughter. Though she'd never met Mona or Mr. Bud, as he was called around Hembree, she knew who they were. Mona had to have been very young at the time. She'd heard Ellis speak of her. They were about the same age. So, why had Amos taken it upon himself to send Mona—in San Diego, no less—monthly stipends of three hundred and fifty dollars, a considerable sum for the time? "Board, lodging, medical expenses," she repeated. She set the document aside and sipped her whiskey, then reaching for the file, thumbed again through the folders inserted in front and in back of the curious bundle of blank paper. There was nothing there. She paused to glance at her watch. It was six-thirty. Though, in the last hour and a half, she'd learned very little about the Eldridge clan, that one little tidbit was enough to rouse her curiosity. Who was she kidding? Her curiosity was already plenty roused. But recalling Dot's reminder about her eight-thirty appointment, she decided to suspend her search till the following day when, with Dot there to answer questions and fill in gaps, it would move along more quickly. She downed the rest of her whiskey, put on her shoes, and headed out, leaving the contents of the file spread across her desk and the mahogany table.

Chapter Nineteen

November 5, 9:15 a.m.
The Tavernette

Olivera got to the Tavernette to find that Springer and Reagan had arrived ahead of him and were sitting at the bar.

Springer waved. "Over here, Chief."

"I'll be right there." He headed toward the hostess station in the dining room, tipped his hat to Ms. Tisdale, whose tight sheath and fishnet stockings seemed all the more inappropriate at nine fifteen in the morning. "Is Ruby in today?"

"She is. Shall I get her for you, Lieutenant?"

"I'd appreciate it if you would."

"She hasn't gotten herself in trouble with the law, has she?" She leaned in slightly and batted her lashes.

He stepped back. "Oh, no. I just wanted to ask her a few questions."

"Hold on a minute." She swished away toward the kitchen.

Olivera returned to the bar and dragged up a stool. "You bring the photographs?" he said to Springer.

"Sure did." Springer unzipped his jacket and pulled out an envelope.

"Okay, good. Ms. Tisdale has gone to look for Ruby. You guys want coffee?"

They nodded.

"Black?"

They nodded again.

"Lieutenant Olivera."

He looked up to see Ruby poised under the arch that led into the bar. She walked toward them. "Mavis says you got some questions for me, Lieutenant."

"I sure do, but first, could you bring us some coffee, please, ma'am?"

"Certainly." She took an order pad and pencil from her apron pocket. "How you want it?"

"Black."

"I'll be right back with that."

"So, I guess," Springer said, looking almost pleased, "Dr. McGinnis *still* hasn't been able to come up with anything—I mean on the ID of the victim."

"Springer—" Olivera shook his head. "—when are you going to give that woman a break? She's a fine coroner, goes right by the book."

"Now don't get any ideas about it, Chief. Nothing wrong with a woman being coroner, but you got to wonder what kind of woman enjoys hanging around dead bodies all day."

"I swear, Springer. If you don't beat all. I never once heard you say that when Old Dr. McGinnis was in charge."

"You're just sweet on her, Chief, so you don't think about these things."

"Sweet on her. For God's sake."

Ruby arrived with a tray of mugs and a steaming pot of coffee and poured three servings. "Can I get you anything else? The kitchen's open if you want somethin' to eat."

"What I'd appreciate is your taking a look at this." He took the envelope from Springer and pulled out a photograph.

"Sure, Lieutenant," she answered with a smile. "Always glad to help out the law if I can."

"But, Ruby, I need to tell you something." He held the image to his chest. "This isn't exactly what you're used to looking at. It was taken of a victim."

"A victim." Ruby cocked her head.

"You probably heard about the man who was found dead earlier this week."

"I sure 'nough did." She frowned. "Read about it in the paper."

"We haven't been able to identify him, so I'm showing this to a few locals. If he's from around here—or maybe even if he isn't—he's likely to have been in the Tavernette at some time or another. We thought you might recognize him."

"Well, you know I don't always look at people close up like."

Olivera handed her the front view.

"Uh-huh, uh-huh," she said, "I do think I seen him a time or two. He's not one of the regulars, I mean he ain't here ever' day, and I don't think he's been around all that long."

"Do you know his name?"

"Oh, my, Lieutenant. I don't always know my own." She laughed.

"Or maybe you know something about him," Springer intervened, "like who he comes in with or where he sits."

"Yeah." She nodded. "I think I seen him with some of the college folks."

"Like Robert Ellison, Hugh Jessup?" Olivera asked.

"No, I don't think he's part of that crowd." She tilted her glasses up. "I can see close up better without my specs."

"Take your time, Ruby."

"This poor old dead fellow—" She blinked her eyes and squinted. "—sorta favors that guy used to come in here."

"Yes?"

"He's been around here a long time. He's one of that Eldridge bunch, but I hardly see the Eldridges now, not the older ones leastwise. They moved to Vicksburg, Mississippi, so I heard."

"This man, the victim, looks to you like the Eldridges?"

"Yeah, he favors 'em quite a bit. You know how it is. Some families look alike, and some, you'd never guess."

"Did you ever see this man, the victim, with any of the Eldridges?"

She shook her head. "No, don't believe so. I'd remember if I had, 'cause when that young Eldridge fellow shows up, we waitresses take to a corner."

"What do you mean?"

"He gets drunker'n Cootie Brown, Lieutenant, if the bartender'll let him. I don't wait on him no more unless I have to."

"Okay, Ruby, that's helpful." Olivera returned the photographs to the envelope. "I tell you what, if you should remember anything about the victim or that other man, would you please let me know?" He handed her his card. "You've got my number right there. Okay?"

"I will. I surely will." She slipped the card into her

apron pocket.

Olivera placed a twenty on the tray. "Keep the change. I appreciate your help."

The men finished their coffee, and Springer and Reagan stayed behind while Olivera spoke with Mavis Tisdale, who'd been watching from the hostess station.

"Ms. Tisdale, I'd like to show you a photograph of a man we're trying to identify, if you've got a minute."

"Certainly, I'll be right with you," she called back as she escorted a couple who'd just arrived into the dining area. She returned promptly. "So how can I help?"

He pulled out the photograph again. "This is a post-mortem photograph of the victim of an assault, looks like. But he didn't have any identification on him."

She held the photograph at arm's length. "Yes, he does look familiar."

"Take a look at this other view." He passed her the profile.

"I'm pretty sure I've seen him, but I couldn't tell you who he is to save my life."

"Ruby said about the same—" He tucked the photographs into the folder. "—but she also thought he looked like another one of your customers."

"Who's that?"

"One of the Eldridges, one of the younger Eldridges. I don't suppose you would have picked up on that?"

"Let me look again."

He handed her back the front view of the victim.

"Yeah, I know who she's talking about. Johnny Eldridge."

"So, you notice a resemblance, too?"

"Maybe. It's kind of hard to tell from this."

"One more thing. Ruby thought this young Eldridge

was a bit of a trouble-maker, drinks too much. Is that your impression?"

"Oh, yeah. If this man were anything like Johnny Eldridge, I mean behavior-wise, we'd all remember him."

"Thanks, Ms. Tisdale. I appreciate your help. And here's my card, in case you think of something that might help us with the ID."

For the first time in four days, Olivera was feeling hopeful. None of the usual paths were leading anywhere, not fingerprints, not medical records, and McGinnis hadn't been able to light a fire under the DNA technicians, who claimed to be backed up on cases every bit as urgent. He was confident that if Ruby thought she remembered John Doe, he must be a local, though not anyone who'd lived in Hembree for a long time. Her recollection of his coming in with the Blanchard crowd seemed to fit. His clothes were professional but casual. Could be a new hire. Ruby's association of the victim with the Eldridges was also encouraging. It beefed up his theory that the victim was tied to the house and probably the family. Then again, Jack Eldridge had pulled a blank. How could John Doe be an Eldridge if Jack didn't recognize him? He didn't seem like he was lying. Which reminded him. He hadn't heard back from the towboat captains. They'd had time to receive the photographs and reply. So, if Eldridge didn't know the victim and none of the captains knew him… Olivera shook his head. It was a conundrum, indeed.

Blanchard College was a couple of blocks from the Square. He left his car parked at the Tavernette and headed over on foot. He put on his hat and lifted the collar of his jacket. It wasn't cold, but a cool breeze was blowing, rustling the leaves and sending them skittering across the sidewalk. The sky was dazzling blue, and the light seemed to come right off the ground. He'd only been in Hembree a year and a half, but he was feeling attached. Hard not to get attached to a pretty little town. Often when he thought of Hembree, he automatically thought of a very different place, Santa Clara, though he was well past missing his old job. His new sense of being the unchallenged boss was much to his liking. It wasn't power he cared about—and what was power anyway in a little stop-in-the-road like Hembree? It was the freedom to do things his way, to be himself. He doubted the Santa Clara station had changed much. Likely, everyone was still kowtowing to the super. He wouldn't give a plug nickel to cross paths with a one of them, except his old partner Nick. Springer and Reagan were nothing to brag about, but they were good men. Never gave him a minute's trouble. And Eads McGinnis was a fine scientist, a good colleague.

He clipped along till he came to the Blanchard entrance, a simple arch with the name of the college spelled in wrought-iron letters. He headed toward the administration building, thinking he would speak to someone in Personnel. The building, much like Delta Infirmary, was white stucco with a tile roof. Old brick steps bordered by a wrought-iron railing led up to the second floor. Taking the steps by two, he entered and scanned the list of offices on the key. Finding Personnel, Room 220, he continued along the terrazzo tile corridor, also much like the corridors of the Infirmary, till he came to an open door. He removed his hat, adjusted his collar and tie, and went in.

"May I help you?" a young man asked from behind

a wooden counter.

Olivera held out his shield. "Lieutenant Gustavo Olivera, Hembree Police. I would like to speak to the director of Personnel."

"She's in a meeting right now."

"When might she be available?"

"Probably an hour, maybe more."

"Okay. Well, this is urgent. Would it be possible to have her step out of the meeting for just a minute?"

The assistant raised his brow. "I don't know, Lieutenant. I suppose I could text her and see if she answers, but she may have turned off her phone."

"If you would try, I'd appreciate it."

The assistant sent the text and held his phone up for Olivera to see. "Have a seat, Lieutenant." He motioned with his head toward a pew-like bench on the front wall.

Olivera sat and, before he'd had a chance to even look out the window, the director came around the door.

"Lieutenant Olivera?" she asked.

"Yes, ma'am," he said, getting up. "I really appreciate your leaving the meeting. This shouldn't take long."

"Of course. I'm Janet Herman, head of Personnel. Let's step into my office."

He followed her into a spacious room, carpeted, with a large desk against a row of tall windows.

"Nice office you've got here."

"These old buildings have their charm, which sort of makes up for their inconveniences." She sat behind the desk and leaned back. "So what's this about?"

"You may know about the incident this week, Monday it was. A man was found dead on a property on the outskirts of town. There was no identification on the body, and fingerprinting and medical records haven't brought up anything. I've shown a post-mortem photograph of the victim to a few locals to no avail, but this morning, someone at the Tavernette thought she'd seen him among the Blanchard crowd, the professors, staff. So, I'm here on a hunting expedition, on the off chance she's right and you might be able to help. I know this is a gruesome matter, but if you wouldn't mind…"

"I understand, Lieutenant. I would be, well, not *happy* but certainly *willing* to take a look."

He placed the two photographs side by side on the desk.

She shook her head, more of a shudder actually than a shake, and took a deep breath. "I know him."

He withdrew the photographs. "I'm sorry, Ms. Herman." He waited for her to continue.

"His name is Charles Ashby. I was hoping he'd come into work, call, or something. He hasn't been in since Friday. His supervisor waited a couple of days before reporting it to me, not wanting to get him in trouble. I was going to see about filing a missing person's report, but—"

"What can you tell me about Mr. Ashby?" Olivera set his notepad on the desk and searched for his pen.

"You need a pen, Lieutenant?"

"Yes, I seem to have come off without mine."

She opened her desk drawer and pulled out a pen.

"Nice…Blanchard College."

"You can keep it. We have a ton of those around."

"Thanks."

"He came here…last fall I think it was," she said. "Yes, last fall. The Development Office hired him. Highly recommended he was…from a college in

Oregon, seems like it was. He's been an excellent hire. Done some good work for Blanchard in the short time he's been here. That's really all I know about him. I don't see him except at the occasional social event, but if you want to speak to his colleagues…"

"Yes, I would. You see, we don't know anything, really. Not even if his death resulted from a fall or an attack. So, if his colleagues could help fill in some gaps. By the way, would you be able to release his personnel file?"

"Normally, I would not, so I'd have to check with General Counsel."

"Okay, please do. It would help to know next of kin—at least that. Or perhaps you could contact them for us."

"Yes, I don't see a problem with that. I'll get in touch with General Counsel and give them your contact information."

"Here's my card—" He placed it on the desk. "—and could you tell me how to get to the Development Office?"

"It's in the building next to this one. Let me see." She checked the directory. "Founders, Room 18. First floor and to your left."

He thanked Ms. Herman for her help and left for the building next door. Too bad it was nearby. He'd have welcomed more time to think about what he was going to say to Ashby's colleagues.

A little older than the administration building, Founders Hall hadn't received the attention it merited— older buildings seldom did in that part of the world. The interior walls were cracked, the woodwork, clean but in need of refinishing. The light fixtures dated easily from the mid-twentieth century or before. A continuous wash of dreary brownish cream paint covered the walls and ceiling.

To reach Room 18, he'd had to go one flight down. He came to an open door, wide and tall, and looked in at the longish room, narrow, with three metal desks backed up against the outside wall. The frosted windows allowed in no more than a modicum of light. He approached the first desk. "I believe this is the Development Office, is it not?"

"Yes, this is Development. Can I help you?" The young man at the desk seemed to give him a quick once over, likely sizing him up *per* the contribution he might make.

Olivera pulled out his shield. "Lieutenant Gustavo Olivera of the Hembree Police."

"Oh," the man said, his expression resolving into disappointment.

The woman at the next desk, a bit prune-faced, watched stiffly.

Olivera glanced between the occupants of the first and second desks. "I understand that a member of your staff, Charles Ashby, hasn't been into work this week."

"Yes," the man said, "Charles hasn't been in since Friday." He glanced at his colleague, who rose and drew closer.

"Not a word from him," she said, "since last Friday."

"May I get your names, please?"

"This is Marion Crosby, Director of Development, and I'm Joe Gillman, Assistant Director."

"Would you like to have a seat, Lieutenant?" Ms. Crosby gestured toward a row of old straight chairs lined up in front of the desks.

Olivera, accepting her offer, took the end chair. "I'm afraid I have some bad news." He set his hat on the chair beside him. "Mr. Ashby has been found dead."

Ms. Crosby rubbed her chin. "I had a bad feeling about this."

Mr. Gillman dropped down in his chair. "I can't believe it. Charles…dead?" He stared down, then looked up. "How did he die? Can you tell us what happened?"

"First, well…I'm sorry to ask you this, but it would help assure me that we are, indeed, speaking of the same individual, if you would take a look at a postmortem photograph." He laid the profile, then the front view, on Mr. Gillman's desk. "Is this your colleague, Charles Ashby?"

Gillman nodded and turned away.

"Ms. Crosby, do you agree? Is this Charles Ashby?"

"That's Charles."

"I'm very sorry for your loss," he said.

"Thank you, Lieutenant," she said.

Mr. Gillman mumbled something.

"We believe Mr. Ashby died late Sunday or possibly early Monday, and we think his death might have come as a result of an assault. If you would help us out by answering a few questions…?"

"Certainly," Ms. Crosby spoke up, "whatever we can do."

"Do you know anything—should this prove to be a homicide—that might give us a lead as to motive? Did Mr. Ashby have any conflicts that you know of?"

"Oh, no," she said. "He'd hardly been here long enough to form any relationships, bad or good."

"What about students, alumni, donors, business

people, whoever you come in contact with in your work?"

"No—" She shook her head. "—Charles got along well. He was polite, friendly. Everyone liked him— wouldn't you agree, Joe?"

"I…yes, well. Here at work, he got along with everyone, as far as I know."

"Mr. Gillman, you seem a little hesitant. Are you thinking of anything that perhaps Ms. Crosby wouldn't know about? For example, did you ever see Mr. Ashby socially?"

"We had a beer together several times. Charles didn't know anyone in Hembree, and I felt sorry for him, being here on his own, no family around, no friends."

"Yes," Olivera said, "Hembree can be a lonely place for a newcomer." He cleared his throat. "Did you ever see him socially, Ms. Crosby?"

"Not really. Charles was a bit younger. I guess I saw him at a couple of fundraisers. We have to do that sort of thing a few times each semester."

"And did you notice anything that struck you as unusual?"

"Unusual?" She shook her head.

"Mr. Gillman, did Charles ever discuss his family or possibly a romantic interest?"

"Not with me he didn't," Gillman said, "but I think he might have had a girlfriend back home. He wasn't at all interested in meeting women. I even wondered if he was engaged, but he never said, and I didn't feel I should pry."

"On these occasions when you went out, where did you go?"

"The Tavernette, usually, always at happy hour.

Once we went to Al's. He liked to grab a beer at the end of the week."

Olivera handed Ms. Crosby, then Mr. Gillman, his card. "Okay, I guess that will be all for now. But, please call if you think of anything. Thank you both—" He smiled faintly. "—and, again, I'm very sorry." He picked up his hat and left the building.

Chapter Twenty

By the time Olivera made it back to the station, Springer and Reagan had left for lunch. He headed to the evidence room, where he'd deposited the computer they'd chanced upon at the hovel. He needed to capture an image of the hard drive, then examine the files, but regrettably, the department lacked the necessary technology. McGinnis, however, had state-of-the-art equipment at the morgue, he was pretty sure. He slipped on latex gloves, bagged and labeled the laptop, and shoved it into his briefcase.

"Ms. Hill, I'm running over to the coroner's office. Might be there for a while. If anything comes up, give me a call."

"No instructions for Springer and Reagan?" she asked.

"Actually, you can tell them to put their feet up—rest up for what lies ahead."

"Oh, my, that'll get 'em to thinking." She laughed.

On the way to Delta Infirmary, he phoned the coroner. "Dr. McGinnis, glad I caught you. The computer we picked up at the hovel…I'm hoping you can help me access the files."

"I can do that. When should I expect you?"

"Five minutes. And, by the way, I've identified John Doe."

"How'd you do that?"

"I followed your suggestion."

"Really?"

"I'll tell you when I get there."

For once, when he pushed through the door to the morgue, McGinnis wasn't in her usual pose, i. e., bent over a body. Relaxing at her desk, she was finishing a sandwich.

"You'll never guess what Springer said about you this morning." He laid the bagged laptop on the counter, tossed his hat on the hat rack, and headed for her desk.

She swallowed and took a sip of iced tea. "Nothing Springer says surprises me."

"He was wondering what kind of woman spends her days picking over dead bodies." He tried his best to look serious.

She burst out laughing. "A brilliant, discerning woman?" En route to the counter, she crumpled the sandwich wrapper and tossed it in the trash. "Let's see what we've got." She put on gloves and removed the computer from the plastic bag. "You've got a proper warrant for this, I'm hoping."

"Of course, and as long as it's in continuous custody, we can rummage around as much as we want. But if we run across files unrelated to the case, well…"

"How are we defining 'related'?"

"Judge Hendricks has given us a wide berth," he said. "I'm thinking anything that might lead to a clarification of the crime—suspects, motive."

"I've got to extract the hard drive first." She perched on a stool next to the counter.

"Mind if I watch?"

"You've never done this before?"

"It's been a while." He pulled up a stool and sat.

She opened the computer and, after a perusal of the inner workings, said, "This looks easy. There's only one hard drive."

"Some have more?" he asked.

"Oh, yeah."

"Like how many?"

"Three, four. Next, we need to make a forensic image of the data. You've dusted for prints, I take it."

"Yep."

"Copying shouldn't take long." She glanced over at Olivera. "So, who's our John Doe?"

"Charles Ashby. He worked in the Development Office at Blanchard. He'd been there about a year. No special friends or family in the area, as far as they know. I spoke with his colleagues, Marion Crosby and Joe Gillman. You know them?"

She shook her head. "You said *I* gave you the lead?"

"Yeah, you told me to ask Ruby at the Tavernette. She recognized him from the photograph but didn't know his name. But she'd seen him come in with the Blanchard crowd. I inquired at Personnel. The director recognized him right off. Said he hadn't been into work."

"Did they have any thoughts about how this might have happened?"

He shook his head. "They said he got along well with people. But there was one little thing. Gillman hesitated like maybe he knew something. You know how people are. They don't want to say anything, and then whatever it was they *didn't* say—"

"—turns out to be the valuable clue you needed

them to tell you."

"Exactly. I'll get back over there later, but I was anxious to find out what's on this computer. Are the files ready yet?"

"Should be. Let me disconnect this." She unhooked the cable and moved the computer to her desk. "Pull up a chair if you want."

"I'm fine." He positioned himself at her side.

"I think I'll start with the user's email, the extortionist's medium of choice."

"Medium of choice, eh?"

"Yes, you've heard of scammers stealing client information from banks, credit card companies, that sort of thing. Once they get the target's personal information, such as a username or a password, they tack it onto the message. Makes the recipient think they have something on him or her."

"But the blackmailer would want to cover his hide, right? He'd erase the messages or set up an account that couldn't be traced."

"Possibly, if he's a pro, but a lot of scammers *aren't* professionals." She clicked on the user's email account and highlighted the subject line of a message. "See that?"

"Yes."

"What does it look like?"

"A password."

"Very good," she said. "Whoever got the message saw their password in the subject line and thought, 'What the heck? If they know my password, they can get into my account.' "

"*And* make good on their threat. Huh."

"Looks like we've got five or six of these, right here together."

"Can you open one?"

She clicked on the first message and read aloud: " 'I know this is one of your passwords, so let's get directly to the point. You were drinking the day of the crash. Your best solution is to pay me $5,000. Let's call it protection. Pay it immediately to my address (see below).' " She nodded toward the screen. "That's the address," she said, then continued reading. " 'Just copy and paste. Pay and you will never hear from me again. If you need proof, don't pay, and your answer will be a knock at your door.' "

"Sort of scary."

"Well, yeah. That's the point, isn't it? Let's look at this one." She opened the next message. "Same thing, except for the password."

"Let's see the others."

She clicked on one after the other. "The same threat on all of them…yep."

"Huh," he mumbled. "Crystal clear, if you ask me. He's targeting the tugboat crew. They must have been drinking the day of the crash. Too bad he doesn't say *which* crash."

"No need. Emails date themselves automatically."

"What's the date?"

"May 10, 2009."

"Six months ago."

She nodded. "I remember hearing about that. Happened not long before I got here. The *Captain Jack* ran into a tanker downriver from here."

"Of course," he said, "and a couple of men drowned. You remember which company it was?"

"I don't, but we can look it up. Key 'towboat wrecks, spring 2009,' on your cell."

Olivera did as she suggested. " 'Crew Missing in Towboat Accident.' "

"Does it give the name of the barge line?"

"Eldridge and Son Barge Lines of Vicksburg, Mississippi. Wow. Everything points to the Eldridges. Sunny Banks, the car, the hovel at the back of the property. Ruby noticed a resemblance between Charles Ashby and Jack's son. She specifically mentioned *him*. This *has* to be Johnny's computer. Can you tell who it's registered to?"

She clicked on the icon in the upper left corner. "Martin Eldridge."

"Which one I wonder—father, son, or grandson?"

"Can't tell you that, but it doesn't matter who it's registered to. Fingerprints should tell us who's been using it."

"And I bet we don't have prints on a one of them."

"If the young one's been arrested for public drunkenness—and sounds like he may have been…"

"That's right," he said. "I'll get Springer on it right away. Okay, so I've taken enough of your time. Thanks, Dr. McGinnis." He smiled. "You're a gem—you know that?"

She blushed. "Thanks, Lieutenant. Always glad to help if I can."

"Do you mind if I leave this with you for the time being?" He gestured toward the laptop.

"Course not. You want me to keep looking?"

"If you have time, yes. Thanks." He grabbed his hat from the rack and left.

Chapter Twenty-One

November 5, 4:30 p.m.
Shepherd Realty

Mosey was standing by the coffee pot, about to sample a pecan tart but, instead, turned to Saffron and said, "Why'd you have to tempt me with these?" She covered the plate with a tea cloth and tucked it around the sides.

"*Tempt* you?"

"I'm still stuffed from last night." She poured herself a cup of coffee. "We went to the seafood buffet at the Yacht Club. My lord, it was good."

"What'd you have?"

"Crab legs, étouffée, fried okra, hushpuppies—"

"Stop, girl—" Saffron threw up her hands. "—you're killing me!" She finished off a tart and drank from her water bottle, then, wriggling out of her cubbyhole, headed to the copier. "I don't reckon Robert has heard anything from Lauren Wilson."

"He said she didn't have much to say on the way to the airport, but mark my words, there's more there than meets the eye."

"Like what?" She placed a form under the lid and pushed the button.

Mosey perched on Saffron's desk and put down her cup. "Since when have we had a client come all the way to Hembree to see a specific house and then—"

"—get scared off by a body in the garage?"

Mosey laughed. "When you put it that way…"

"What other way can you put it?"

"The other day at the Tavernette, she seemed worried, like maybe there was something personal about it."

"Personal?"

"Yeah, think about it. All of us involved—you, me, John Earle, even Robert and Hugh—felt sort of… How should I put it?"

"Horrified?"

Mosey laughed. "Of course, we were upset, and, yes, we felt bad for the victim and his family—whoever they may be. I wouldn't say, though, I've been *worried*. I mean, I hope they catch the person and all that, but I don't feel concerned in a personal way. But Lauren *did*— at least it seemed like it to me."

"She say something?" Saffron gathered up her copies and headed back to her desk.

"No, it was more what she didn't say. She was quiet, distracted. I also wonder why she hasn't called by now."

"Maybe you ought to call her, touch base."

"I thought I'd give it a couple of days."

Saffron sat in her chair. "I guess you heard they identified the body."

"Are you kidding me? Who was it?"

"Somebody at the college, but not a professor."

"You got *The Gazette* there?"

"I heard it on the radio."

"Let me see if I can find it on my phone." Mosey went to her office and returned quickly, reading as she approached. "It *is* someone from Blanchard," she said excitedly. " 'The body discovered Monday at Sunny Banks, a vacant property owned by Martin J. Eldridge III, has been identified as Charles Ashby, who held the position of Associate Director of Development at Blanchard College.' "

"You know him?" Saffron said.

"I might have met him, but, no, I don't know him. I wonder if Robert knows him, or Hugh. You ever meet him?"

"Where would I meet him?"

"How should I know?" Mosey picked up her cup and sipped. "But Hembree's pretty small. Seems like somebody would know him. Maybe I ought to call Olivera."

"Now, why would you do that?"

"See if he's got any leads."

"Like what?"

"Suspects, of course. People get offed by people they know. So now that Olivera knows who it was, he'll start questioning his close associates, find out if he had any enemies, search his house…"

"Mosey, you are the last person Gus Olivera wants to hear from." Saffron stapled the forms together and slipped them into her top drawer.

"What do you mean?" Mosey frowned. "He was over here bugging me just yesterday."

Saffron shook her head. "Don't call him. He's probably up to his neck in evidence."

"I don't think so. I bet he doesn't have squat." She slid her phone into her jeans pocket and picked up her cup. Just then, the front door opened. Mosey craned her neck. It was John Earle coming in. "Hey, John Earle."

"Afternoon, Mosey." He deposited his hat on the

hall tree behind the door.

Saffron smiled. "I had a feeling you'd be here."

"How's that?" He stopped in front of her desk.

"You can smell pecan pie a mile off." She pointed toward the kitchenette. "Go on and get a tart and take a couple with you."

"I sure will—" His face brightened. "—but that's not what I'm here for."

"So, why?" Mosey said. "Must be a special occasion."

John Earle rolled his eyes. "Jack Eldridge called me."

Mosey's interest piqued.

"He wanted to ask me about the homicide on his daddy's property. Old Man Eldridge has caught wind of it, and he's a little agitated." His brow dropped.

"Huh," Saffron said, "I'd be, too."

"They finally identified the guy," John Earle said. "I guess y'all heard."

"Yeah, we did," Mosey said.

"So, ladies, what we gonna do about this?" He leaned against Saffron's desk.

"I don't know why you're asking *us*." Saffron rolled back in her chair.

"Well, I gotta ask somebody, and it might as well be you." He looked at one, then the other.

"So what's the interest here, John Earle?" Mosey asked.

"What's the interest?" he repeated.

"You could look at this from a lot of angles," Mosey said. "Like, there's Old Man Eldridge's angle. He's probably wondering why Ashby was killed on *his* property—unless, of course, he knows him, and if he does, he probably has a pretty good idea. He might know who did it."

"Mosey, you have got one twisted mind, girl."

"I don't know why you'd say that." She opted for disbelief, though a smirk hovered slightly below the surface.

"Poor old Martin," he continued, "why would you think he knows the victim?"

"He *might* know him." She crossed her arms and turned away.

"I doubt he's thinking about the dead man," John Earle said. "I imagine he wants to sell his house and car, and he figures this murder has thrown a monkey wrench into the deal."

"And he would be right," Saffron said.

"I don't know what you think *we* can do about it," Mosey said.

"I thought you might have some idea of how we could extricate ourselves and Martin from this mess."

Mosey sighed. "I could call Lauren, see if she's still interested, and if she is, I could call Olivera, see if he has any idea when the court will release the owner's property."

"See there," John Earle said with a smile. "That sounds like a plan. You contact them, and I'll drop by Magnolia, tell Martin we're doing everything we can. And one more thing," he said, holding up his index finger. "Call me soon as you know anything."

"I'm on it, boss." She headed off to her office. "And how's about answering your cellphone for a change?"

He looked at Saffron. "She sounds like my wife."

Saffron cackled.

When Mosey reached her desk, she didn't call

Lauren or Olivera. She called Robert.

"What's up?"

"John Earle's here at the office," she said, "and seems like Old Man Eldridge is upset about the homicide."

"We're calling it a homicide, are we?"

"Who knows?" Mosey said. "But anyway, John Earle wants me to call Lauren, see what she's decided, and then he wants me to call Olivera and find out when the house and car can be sold."

"So?"

"I wanted to clear it with you first."

"I don't see the harm in calling her, but keep it simple. Don't go poking around—"

"I have no intention," she cut in, "of poking around in anything. I'll ask her if she's interested. That's all."

"Once you talk to her, call me back," Robert said. "By the way, did you hear about Charles Ashby?"

"Yeah, everybody's talking about it."

"Did you know him?" Mosey asked with anticipation.

"Not well. I've run into him at receptions—that sort of thing."

"So, what's the talk?"

"Talk?"

"Surely somebody must have *some* idea."

"Yeah, there're some rumors," Robert said.

"What kind of rumors?"

"Somebody saw him arguing with somebody."

"Did they know who the other person was?"

"I don't know. Look, I got to get back to work, but you be careful what you say to Lauren."

"I will."

"And call me."

Mosey hung up and bounced back toward reception. "I just talked to Robert. There's a rumor that somebody saw Ashby arguing with somebody."

"It wasn't you, was it?" John Earle said.

He and Saffron cracked up.

"Very funny," Mosey said with a smirk. "I've got an idea."

"Oh, no, here it comes." John Earle slinked toward the kitchenette, hands covering his head.

"What if *we*—you and me," Mosey said, turning to Saffron, "drop by the Magnolia to see Uncle T. Patrick, take him some pecan tarts?"

"Would you leave my uncle out of this?" Saffron waggled her head.

"I'm not involving him in anything, but while we're there, I'll drop by Old Man Eldridge's room, say I'm the agent assigned to Sunny Banks—"

"—which is a lie," Saffron cut in.

"It's hardly a lie. I *have* shown the place."

"You're not the agent. It's not even listed."

"Never mind that. If I could talk to him, maybe I could find out what's got his dander up."

John Earle stepped out of the kitchenette with a tart in one hand, a cup of coffee in the other. "Mosey, that is a terrible idea, and you stay away from there, ya hear?"

"Of course, John Earle," Mosey said, fingers crossed behind her back, "whatever you say."

"I thought you were going to call Lauren," Saffron said.

"Later."

Chapter Twenty-Two

November 5, 2:00 p.m.
Hembree Police Station

Olivera was in a heat, and his urge was to be alone
with his thoughts, sit down at his desk, take a look at his
evidence board, see what he had. With a little time to
think, maybe he could figure out where to go from there.
He'd been stuck for days, spinning his wheels. But now,
unexpectedly, the case had picked up steam. He knew
who the victim was and, accordingly, had something to
work with. The oddly silent stage, as he thought of it, had
come to life. The victim had a name, even if Ashby's
associates knew little about him. Yes, he thought,
nodding, *finally*, the victim had a name.

The evidence board hung on the partition by his
desk. He'd pinned up the post-mortem photographs and
the snapshots of Sunny Banks and Martin Eldridge's
sedan. He printed "Charles Ashby" on a tab and stuck it
to the board. Below the pictures of the property, he'd
added snaps of the hovel and gum brake. He printed
"computer" and "files" on two more tabs and tacked
them below the picture of the hovel. He added two final
tabs, "extortion" and "towboat crash," and, using a
string, attached them to "computer" and "files." He
stepped back to take a look. He didn't know when he'd
seen so many developments in a single day. He had little

on the victim, but a good bit on the house and property.

He needed to speak to Springer. "Come in here a second, would you, Springer?"

He came in right away, tablet in hand.

"I need you to do a couple of things." He sat, then pushed back in his chair. "Uh, first, did you get any prints off the steering wheel?"

"You know, Chief—" He scratched his head. "—I didn't, but I'll—"

"And the number on the desk pad?"

"Not yet."

"You can get it off the board—" Olivera pointed. "—and the computer—you checked the case for prints, right?"

"I did, but you know what, Chief?"

"What?"

"There wasn't a print on it anywhere. Wiped clean."

"Well, that's unfortunate." Olivera rubbed his chin. "Turns out it's registered to Martin Eldridge. We've started checking the files, Dr. McGinnis and I." He reared back. "Guess what we found in one of the email accounts."

"I have no idea, Chief."

"Messages with passwords in the subject line."

"Passwords."

"Turns out—Dr. McGinnis knew this, I didn't—blackmailers use passwords to trick their victims into thinking they know something. The perp was trying to extort money, looks like, but we don't know for sure who the perp is. Fingerprints on the computer might have told us."

Springer closed his tablet and stuck it back in his shirt pocket.

"You know, that is really weird, Springer. No finger prints on the computer..." He leaned back. "And one more thing." He tilted his head toward the evidence board. "I've been updating this. We've got the victim's name but know little about him. I need to run back to Blanchard, question Ashby's colleagues again. But first things first. Get me his address. We'll need a warrant, and as soon as I get it, we'll head over. I want you and Reagan to go with me."

Springer turned to leave, then stopped. "You want the address first?"

"Yes, get it for me, please."

He watched as Springer's broad shoulders disappeared around the partition. Then he rolled toward the evidence board. He'd divided it into three sections, one each for the victim, the place, and suspects. That empty third section was vexing. He hadn't a single suspect, only a couple of "people of interest," i. e., Jack Eldridge and his son Johnny. He'd take a close look at both, but before he did that, he needed more information on the victim. He reached for an index card and printed, "Ashby, who was he?" If he had a better idea of who, *diablos*, he was, he might be able to figure out who wanted him dead.

"Chief." Springer peeked around the partition. "I got an address for Ashby. It's 712 West Payne Street. His full name, in case you want to know, is Charles Duncan Ashby."

Olivera unpinned the victim's name, picked up another index card, and printed. He tossed the pen aside. "Let's see if I can speak to Judge Hendricks. Sit tight," he said as he rose. "I ought to be back in half an hour or so." He left the cubicle and strode across the floor, slipping his arms into his sports coat as he went.

About a half hour later, Olivera gave Springer a call. "I've got the warrant. I'll swing by for you and Reagan. Wait for me outside with the usual supplies."

"Okay, Chief. No cones, I guess."

"No cones, just bags and the evidence gathering paraphernalia."

Shortly after, they arrived at Ashby's home, a modest stucco house three blocks off the south side of the Square. Olivera pulled up in the gravel drive, which ended at a one-car garage at the back of the lot. He brought the squad car to a halt near the front door and walked up three steps to the entrance. To the right of the door, the mailbox had spilled over, and several newspapers lay on the stoop. He opened the screen door and jiggled the knob. "It's locked," he yelled back to Springer. "Want to see if you can open this?" He jiggled it again.

"Let's see if the old credit card trick works." Springer inserted a plastic card and, slowly turning the knob, dragged the card in his direction. "It's working. So, if the deadbolt isn't set, and I don't think it is…" He pushed, and the door gave to his touch.

"Reagan," Olivera said, "you go around to the back and wait at the door, assuming there is one. And take a quick look around. See if you can see anything suspicious."

Olivera and Springer entered the living room, which was dark and sparsely furnished. Olivera slipped on gloves, then flicked the light switch. There weren't any paintings or pictures on the walls, no knickknacks, nothing of a personal nature. The wood floor was bare, not even a rug in front of the sofa, which was gray and worn. "Must have picked that up at a garage sale." A knock came at the back, and he turned to Springer. "Let Reagan in, would you?"

Springer passed through the dining room into the kitchen. "See anything out there?" he asked as he opened the door.

"A garbage can," Reagan said.

"No car in the garage?" Springer asked.

"Nope."

"Now that's interesting."

"What's interesting?" Olivera stood at the door to the kitchen.

"There's not a car in the garage, Chief."

"So where's Ashby's car?" Olivera said. "You'd think he'd have one."

"Huh," Springer said, "funny we didn't think of that before."

"You know," Reagan said, "I've been thinking all along, Lieutenant, that this Ashby fellow went over there to see the house. But maybe he didn't."

Springer's eyes grew big. "Yeah…maybe he went to see the car."

"Could be," Olivera said.

"Maybe he didn't own a car," Reagan said.

"Or maybe he had an old beater," Springer said, "and wanted to upgrade to a Tyche-XL500."

"Doesn't this beat all?" Olivera sighed. "We don't even know if he owned a car."

"Yeah," Reagan said, "we don't know beans."

"So, we'd better get to looking," Olivera said. "Close the door, Reagan, and start with the kitchen. Springer, check the dining and living rooms, and I'll check the bedroom. Look for documents, photographs, anything to help us establish his identity—medical history, work history, social. Open all drawers and cabinets. You know the drill."

Reagan and Springer put on gloves and began searching their assigned rooms. The familiar clatter of an investigation—the opening and closing of cabinets and drawers, the shuffling of paper—rose behind Olivera as he headed to the bedroom, adjacent to the living room. He started with the victim's closet, ran his hand along the scant collection of slacks, shirts, and sports coats that hung from the rod. The victim's shoes—loafers, slip-ons, and running shoes—were neatly arranged on a rack at the bottom. The shelf at the top was stacked with boxes. "Might as well start there," he mumbled. He pulled down a stack of boxes and set it on the bed, which was unmade, but the linens looked fresh. He sniffed. The room smelled of nothing, not even cologne. He removed the box tops, and shoes rolled out: moccasins, tennis shoes, oxfords, all new. He stuffed the shoes back in the boxes and lifted down the second stack. He opened the box on top. "Aha…documents." He emptied the contents onto the dresser. "Exactly what I was hoping for." He stepped to the living room door. "Springer, let's organize as we go. Box any documents and label them as to room and location. And bring me a box, please."

"How big?"

"Middle-size will do."

"What you got, Chief?" Springer grabbed a folded box and, opening it, followed Olivera into the bedroom.

"Insurance papers, looks like. Renter's insurance, car insurance." He held up an envelope. "So that settles that."

"He *did* have a car," Springer said.

Olivera opened the envelope and pulled out a form.

"Huh," Springer grunted. "So where in Sam Hill is it? It wasn't at the death scene."

"Which might mean it's at the crime scene."

"And where's that?" Springer asked.

"I wish I knew. The car might lead us to it."

"I reckon it could." Springer nodded. "Suppose, just suppose, Chief, that Ashby drove to the house to check out old Martin's Tyche. Took it for a spin, brought it back to the house. Then later on, after the perp killed Ashby, the perp drove off in Ashby's car."

"Yep, could have happened that way. But what about the perp's car? By the way, Springer. How far have you gotten with the fingerprints?"

"Not far. You called just as I was about to—"

"So you don't know," he interrupted, "if we have prints for Johnny Eldridge?"

"I'll take care of it soon as we get back."

Chapter Twenty-Three

November 5, 5:00 p.m.
Magnolia Nursing Home

"Uncle T. is gonna be mighty glad to get these." Saffron tucked the last of the pecan tarts into a container and closed the lid. "But I'm not a bit proud of our reason for going over there."

"Wait a minute. You said you were saving the pecan tarts for Uncle T."

"Yes, but I was *not* figuring on providing you with a cover."

"He doesn't have to know, and he'll be plenty glad to see you. Have you talked to him since the funeral?"

"Sorry to say I haven't."

"How'd he take Eugene's death?"

"Well, it was a consolation to meet his family."

"At least some good came of that awful ordeal," Mosey said. "Shall we drive over in my truck? I can drop you back here."

"No, I'll drive. It may take you a while to wheedle something out of Old Man Eldridge. You'd better let Robert know not to expect you—"

"Are you kidding?" Mosey cut in. "No way am I phoning Robert." She picked up her tote and headed out the door. "I'll see you there," she called back.

"By the way," Saffron yelled across the parking lot,

"did you talk to Lauren?"

Mosey shook her head. "I left a message."

Getting to the nursing home ahead of Saffron, Mosey decided to call Lauren while she waited. "Lauren, hi, this is Mosey."

"Mosey, good to hear from you."

"I wanted to touch base since we sort of left things dangling."

"I wish I could have finalized my plans."

"You still can if you decide on one of the other houses, I mean besides Sunny Banks."

"I sort of had my heart set on it, but now—"

"I know. The house is surely stigmatized. I don't know if that would make a difference to you, but for the time being, it can't be sold, not until the court releases it."

"Any idea how long that will take?"

"Not really. I could speak to Lieutenant Olivera if you want, see if they're getting anywhere."

"I wouldn't want to put you to any trouble."

"It's no trouble. I'll give him a call and let you know."

Mosey slipped the phone in her tote. She'd avoided mentioning that they'd identified the victim. She couldn't see how getting into details with Lauren would improve matters. A knock came at her window. Saffron was peeping in. Mosey opened the door. "I talked to Lauren."

"What'd she say?"

"Still thinking about Sunny Banks."

"Well, Sunny Banks may be out of the question."

"Why?" Mosey lifted her brow. "They'll release it sooner or later."

"She can't wait on that house, girl." Saffron shook her head. "Who knows when they'll solve the case?"

"Well, we can help them along," Mosey said with a knowing smile.

"Which is exactly what we're doing here."

They crossed the lot and entered the lobby. Sunlight beamed in from a row of long windows in front of reception. "Hi," Saffron said to the receptionist. "I'm here to see my uncle, Mr. T. Patrick Brown. Could you let him know I'm here? I'm Saffron Smiley, his niece."

"Is he expecting you?"

"He is. I called a little while ago."

"Okay, let me check with the attendant on the ward."

"And I—" Mosey caught the receptionist's attention. "—am here to see Mr. Martin Eldridge, on a business matter. I called ahead."

"Yes," she said, "the attendant will bring him shortly. You ladies can wait on the sun porch, if you like."

They headed to the sun porch off reception, a long room with white wicker chairs, high back rockers, and cushions upholstered in flowered polished cotton. "You want to sit over there?" Mosey motioned toward a settee.

"Sure, but we should separate. You sit on that end. I'll sit right here."

"Why so far apart?" Mosey said, arms akimbo.

"I don't want Uncle T. to figure out what we're up to. If you're down there—"

"So, I can't say hi to Uncle T?"

Saffron rolled her eyes. "Just take care of business, and let me visit with my uncle."

Saffron watched as Mosey huffed off toward the end of the room and, picking up a magazine, sat in a rocker next to the window.

With the arrival of Uncle T., pushed in by a petite attendant, Saffron stood to give her uncle a hug. "Uncle T. You're looking wonderful."

"Oh, I'm sure I look just peachy." He wiped his mouth with a handkerchief, folded it, and slipped it in his breast pocket.

"You're all dressed up," she said in justification of her earlier comment.

He stretched out his arms, displaying the sleeves of his tweed jacket. "This old thing?"

"Now, Uncle T.," she said, sitting back down, "that jacket's brand new. Momma gave it to you for your birthday."

"I don't remember nothing no more," he said with a sigh.

"Look what I brought you." She pulled a pecan tart out of her tote and unwrapped it. "You want one now?"

"I ain't very hungry, but I 'spect I could eat half."

She broke it in half and placed it on a napkin.

He bit into it and chewed. "Yeah, that's good. You a good cook, Saffron, or did you buy that at the sto'?"

"Uncle T., since when did I ever bring you store-bought pastries?"

He chuckled. "I thought that'd get a rise out of you."

Meanwhile, Martin J. Eldridge III arrived, escorted by a male attendant. "Are you Ms. Frye?" the attendant asked Saffron.

"No, I'm not." She pointed her pompadour toward Mosey.

"Oh, okay, sorry." He offered his arm to the tall man at his side, who seemed not at all pleased.

"I am perfectly capable, sir—" He shook his arm

away. "—of walking a few feet on my own steam." He jabbed the carpet with his cane, a simple carved ebony stick with a plain pewter handle.

"I know, Mr. Eldridge, but it doesn't hurt to have someone to lean on."

"Huh!" He took a few more steps.

Mosey rose to meet him and extended her hand.

"I can't shake hands with you left-handed, miss," he said, "but if you wanted to kiss me on the cheek, that'd be appreciated."

Mosey laughed. "Mr. Eldridge, I don't think we know each other quite that well. I'm Mosey Frye. I'm an agent with Shepherd Realty. I'm here on business…on behalf of Mr. Shepherd."

"John Earle, yes. I know who you mean."

"Shall we have a seat over here?"

The attendant helped him get seated. "I'll leave you two alone. Call me if you need anything," he said to Mosey.

Mosey took out a business card and placed it on the table in front of Mr. Eldridge. "I understand you have some concern about your property—the house and car."

"Yes, I'm concerned. Of course, I'm concerned," he said, raising his voice. "That was our home where they found that man…dead, murdered maybe, and in my car, of all places," he boomed. His thin skin turned pink, and his veins stood out at his temples.

"I know it's been a shock. A person never expects anything like that to happen on their own property, but I can assure you, Mr. Eldridge, the house is fine. No harm done."

"No harm done?" His look was one of astonishment, as if what Mosey had said was purely ludicrous.

"We're doing all we can," she said, "to see this is resolved quickly. I'm sure the house will sell without any loss of value."

He shook his head and poked the carpet with his cane.

"That's a nice cane you've got there, Mr. Eldridge."

His attention shifted—as she'd hoped it would—to his cane, which he laid across his lap, then said, looking Mosey in the eye, "You interested in these old things?"

"Yes, I am. My grandfather had a fine collection, not that he ever used one, but he liked the looks of them. So do I. He had one with an artfully carved wolf's head with moonstones for eyes."

"Moonstones, eh? Well, I don't have anything like that, but I do have a bunch of these." He held it up. "My grandson loved to play with them when he was a kid." He laughed. "He thought he was a knight and this was his sword." While he spoke, he twisted the cane back and forth, as if he were imagining his grandson at play.

"My friend Nadia Abboud has an antique shop. I bet she'd be glad to take them off your hands, should you be interested."

His chin dropped. "Well, they've taken just about everything."

"They have?" Her expression wilted into a frown.

"My house, car, all the furniture."

"That must have been when you and your wife came here to live."

He nodded. "They had an estate sale, but I didn't like the idea. The sale should come *after* you're dead, and I'm not dead, not yet."

"Of course, not," she agreed. "You're far from dead." She came close to patting him on the arm but didn't want to encourage any misbehaving.

"My kin folks seem to think so." His eyes looked wild. "They've hauled off all our belongings, except this cane and a few suits of clothes."

"I'm sure your son must have your interest at heart."

He shook his head again, apparently unconvinced.

"Did you know, Mr. Eldridge, that my grandfather and father were your attorneys? And now, my Aunt Carlotta has taken over the firm. You can trust her and your son Jack to look after things for you."

His eyes glided from the cane to Mosey's face. "So you're Ellis's daughter?"

"I am."

"I'll be. Old Amos and I were huntin' buddies." His head nodded gently.

She smiled and chattered on, not sure where she wanted to take the conversation. What could Eldridge know that might shed light on the death of Charles Ashby? She hadn't a clue. All she knew was what John Earle had told her, that Martin was concerned about his property. So, she boldly asked something that felt a little risky. She hadn't wanted to mention the dead man's name, but with no other idea of how to steer the conversation in a productive direction, she said, "Mr. Eldridge, you know all this is going to be cleared up as soon as they figure out if it was a homicide and, if so, who might have had motive to end poor Mr. Ashby's life."

"Yes, I imagine so, and I guess they don't know either one yet."

"Not as far as I've read in the paper. I don't suppose you have any thoughts on the subject."

He cocked his head. "Well, I do know a couple of

fellows who had it in for us Eldridges. When you're in bid'ness, people sometimes figure they can wring some money out of you."

"Are you referring to your barge lines?"

"Of course I am—what else?" He punctuated his words with a punch of the cane. He rubbed the handle with scrawny fingers and let his head wobble from side to side, as if he were on a tugboat himself, plowing through the waters of a great river. "We Eldridges, we always earned our living on the river. And, ya see, some crew member would come after us over some incident or another. The river is risky. If they wanted a sweet, safe job, they ought not to have come on it in the first place."

"So you think this incident could have had something to do with your business?"

He nodded slowly. "Maybe…possibly…"

"You can't think of any other reason?"

He faced Mosey head on. "Yes, ma'am, actually, I can, but that was a long, long time ago."

She was taken aback by this semi-confession of something other than business, maybe something family related that might have ruffled the waters. "In the way of retribution, you mean?" She'd suddenly remembered her conversation with Carlotta.

"I can't rule it out."

"And you said a long, long time ago."

"Yes, it was," he said, "and I've been thinking about that lately. You know sometimes you make an enemy and he never goes away. Never goes away but never shows his ugly face, either."

"Mr. Eldridge—" She sat forward. "—if you know something, it might be to your advantage to speak to Lieutenant Olivera. It might hurry the case along, help

175

put all this behind you, so you could sell the house and car free and clear."

He shook his head. "Some things you can never put behind you. They seem to follow you all your days." He wiped his eyes and looked at Mosey. "Miss, I'm feeling a little tired. I think I'll go back to my room."

"Of course, let me get the attendant for you." Not wanting to leave him alone, she motioned to the receptionist. "Mr. Eldridge would like to go back to his room." It was then that she noticed Saffron had slipped out ahead of her. She hadn't even gotten to speak to Uncle T.

The attendant arrived, and Mosey, after saying goodbye to Mr. Eldridge, walked down the steps and across the gravel parking lot to her truck. She pulled out her phone, about to call John Earle, but before she could tap in the number, a voice, her father's voice, sounded a familiar warning.

Mosey, stay away from Waite House, ya hear.

"Waite House! Don't you mean Sunny Banks?"

The voice came again—*Stay away from Waite House.*

"What's this got to do with Waite House?"

He didn't answer.

Mosey drove back into town, and feeling like she needed to talk to somebody—share the vagaries to which Old Man Eldridge had alluded—she rounded the Square a couple of times. Slowing down, she looked up at the windows on the second floor of the Frye Building. They were dark. "Phooey," she uttered and drove on. "I wonder if Nadia's still at the store." She took Lee Street at the corner and drove to Nadia's shop, parked, and hurried toward the entrance. The door was locked, and the sign said "closed." The lights were on, though. She knocked repeatedly. "Nadia, you here? It's me, Mosey."

"I'm coming. Hold your horses," came a voice from inside. A second later, Nadia opened the door. "What's up?"

"Thank goodness you're here." Mosey entered, paced the length of the counter, then turned to face Nadia. "You remember the other day I was telling you about how Daddy talks to me sometimes?"

Nadia's brows elevated slightly. "Of course, I remember. It's not every day your best friend tells you she converses with ghosts."

"For heaven's sake. It's not a ghost. It's just my daddy's voice. You know."

"I *don't* know."

"Okay, forget about that part. I was over at the nursing home—Saffron and I. She was taking some pecan tarts to Uncle T., but that was just a ruse, well, in part. Actually, we went over there mainly so I could talk to Old Man Eldridge."

Nadia rolled her eyes.

"What?" Mosey said.

"What tomfoolery have you been up to now?"

"Nadia, you just whoosh that thought right out of your head." She grabbed Nadia's feather duster and brushed it back and forth across the back of a tallish chair.

"Whatever." Nadia grabbed the feather duster and dropped it in an antique crock behind the door.

"So, anyhow. I wanted to talk to him to see if he had any ideas about why somebody might have had it in for Charles Ashby. You know he's the dead man, right?"

"So I heard."

"We talked for a while, and he opened up a little. He's worried about his house and car, which is understandable. John Earle thought it was just the business transaction he was concerned about. But I think it's more than that. He's thinking somebody is taking revenge. Like maybe somebody who was injured on one of his towboats—who knows? Or it might be a relative of a deceased crew member. Tugboats sink every now and again."

"You think that could be it, revenge against the Eldridges?"

"Not exactly," she said as she dropped into a wingchair. "It couldn't be *exactly* that—Charles Ashby wasn't an Eldridge." She frowned. "But there's more to the story. Right at the end, I asked if he could think of anything else, and he said, yes, he could, but *that*—whatever *that* was—had happened a long time ago. Then he said he was tired and wanted to go back to his room."

"Poor old fellow." Nadia sat in the chair across from Mosey. "I don't know how you had the nerve to hassle that old man."

"I wasn't hassling him. It's to his advantage that Olivera get to the bottom of this."

"If you say so," Nadia said with a sigh.

"But listen." Mosey sat forward. "I'm coming to the important part. Just as I was crossing the parking lot, I heard Daddy say, 'Stay away from Waite House.' And I said, 'Waite House? Don't you mean Sunny Banks?' And he said the same thing again, 'Stay away from Waite House.' "

"Bizarre."

"Yeah, it *is* bizarre, or maybe it isn't. Maybe there's some connection." She got up and paced. "There's no apparent connection, but maybe there *is* a connection."

"Like what?"

"Well, the Waites and the Eldridges are two old families around here. They must have known each other. Maybe there's something in their past we don't know about. But the part I can't figure is how Charles Ashby was involved. He's not from here. He's only been here a year. I doubt he knew the Eldridges or the Waites."

"So why was he over there?"

"I've assumed he went to look at the car or the house. Both are up for sell."

"Yeah, this is a tough one."

"I need to talk to Dot or Carlotta. They're the only people I know who might have some notion about this."

"I'm ready to close up." Nadia stood. "You want to stop somewhere for a drink?"

"Yeah, I could use one. And I'm buying." She smiled and gave Nadia a hug. "Nadia you are a good, good friend. I don't know what I would do without you."

"Uh-huh." Nadia turned out the lights and stepped out on the sidewalk. "Oh, wow, Mosey. Look at that harvest moon."

Chapter Twenty-Four

Friday, November 6, 8:00 a.m.
Frye, Frye, and Humphrey

The following day, Carlotta got to the office earlier than usual. "Oh, Dot," she said, a little breathless, "I'm so glad you're here." She pushed the door closed, walked quickly past Dot's desk and into her office.

"Why, Carlotta, I'm always here by eight. You know that."

"Come in here for a second, please, ma'am."

"Hold on," Dot said. "You want some coffee?"

"No, that'll wait. I want to show you something."

Dot slipped her swollen feet into her black leather pumps and toddled in, a slight look of apprehension on her seamlessly powdered face. As it was early in the work day, her rouge was perfectly set, and the subtle rose of her lips blushed tidily within the lines.

Seated on the edge of her desk, Carlotta was holding a hanging file in her hand. "Take a look at this, if you don't mind."

Dot approached, her anxiety apparently heightened. "Oh, my, what did I do?"

Carlotta laughed. "Dot, hon, this isn't about you. You haven't done a thing." She reached out and patted her on the arm.

"No?" She moaned. Her sloping shoulders sloped

lower. "Carlotta, you scared me to death."

"I'm sorry. I didn't mean to. I've been thinking about this half the night, and I know you can explain it. I have no idea—"

"About what?" she cut in. The tips of her fingers, resting on Carlotta's desk, suddenly tensed. Poor Dot! She looked like a big, fluffy cat that, able neither to flee nor fight, had simply frozen.

"This crazy file," Carlotta said. "Look." She opened it, and legal pads and typing paper spilled out onto the desk and floor. "What's all this?"

"Well, I don't know." She picked up a legal pad from the floor. "It looks like a bunch of old paper."

"And look at this. 'Family Lines,' you see that?" Carlotta pointed to the green label.

"So?"

"This entire file contains nothing but a bunch of blank paper and one letter unrelated in any way I can see to Eldridge and Son Barge Lines."

"What does the letter say?" Dot asked, her voice trembling.

Carlotta fished out the letter from the pile, then proceeded to read the missive that Amos Frye had written to Hamilton Waite several decades before. When finished, she reached for the hanging file and sat toggling it and the letter back and forth. "What does one have to do with the other? Can you explain that to me?"

Dot's perfectly groomed brows shot up. "When was all that?"

Carlotta glanced back at the letter. "February 15, 1970. And, Dot—" She stood. "—there is no point in stalling. You know perfectly well what this is about. Your initials are on the bottom of the letter."

"Then I must have typed it, but that doesn't prove I was privy to—" Dot stopped and shook her head.

"Stop playing possum with me, and tell me what this is about."

"I think I heard the coffee pot go off. Let me get you a cup. I wouldn't mind one myself." She padded out, leaving Carlotta sputtering for words.

"Okay, you win. But when you come back in here, you're going to explain this, you hear?"

"I hear," Dot called back.

Carlotta slumped down into one of the upholstered chairs and waited for Dot's return.

The minute hand on the old wall clock advanced a fraction, and Dot came back with two cups on a tray. "Now then," she said, setting the tray in front of Carlotta. "Let me say from the get-go that Amos and Ellis had nothing to do with this. You got that?" Having led with her strong suit, she relaxed a little.

"I got it."

"They got dragged into something—well, it was not their problem, but all the same—"

"Dragged into what?" Carlotta sat up straight. The more Dot hedged, the more agitated she became.

"It was a personal matter," Dot said, "and Amos wanted a record of it, but he wanted it sort of hidden, and I came up with the idea of putting it in among the Eldridge files. The Eldridges, after all, were at the heart of it."

"The heart of what?"

"I'm coming to that." She sat in the chair most distant from Carlotta. "You see—" She reached for her cup. "—Mona Waite—gosh, she was only about twenty at the time—got herself into some trouble."

"Trouble. You mean she was pregnant?"

Dot blushed and lowered her head. "Yes, she was."

"So, who was the father?"

Dot breathed deep. "Her daddy insisted *Ellis* was the father, but he wasn't. She and Ellis had a few dates, but he was an honorable man. You know that."

"Of course."

"Finally it came out—not publicly, of course—that Mona had gone to California, where she had some friends, friends of the family, I think it was. And she stayed out there till she had the baby. She placed it for adoption, privately, then came back to Hembree."

"So, why did my step-father write this letter to Hamilton Waite?"

"Mona finally admitted to Ellis—and her parents, too—who the daddy was, mainly because she didn't want Ellis to feel like she'd left him holding the bag. Of course, he knew already *he* wasn't the father. It was Amos, then, who spoke to the boy's daddy and recommended *he* pay her expenses. She didn't want to ask her daddy for the money and even if she had, I'm not sure he would have given it to her. So, Amos oversaw the payments. The paternal grandfather deposited the money in an account, and Amos wrote the checks and sent them to Mona."

"May I ask who the father was?"

Dot sighed. "Can't you guess?"

"Well, the letter is in the Eldridge files, so I'd have to guess it was an Eldridge. Surely not Martin Sr."

"No, it wasn't Martin. It was his young son Jack."

"Oh, my. Jack Eldridge got Mona Waite pregnant."

Dot nodded and sipped her coffee. She set the cup down. "But, Carlotta, don't you tell a soul, because in all

183

these years I have never told anyone. Not that it would really matter much now. Everybody involved is gone from here, either to their grave or to another town."

"Oh, Dot, I'm not sure that's true."

Dot stared back, eyes wide.

"What happened to Mona?"

"She finished law school, got married, and never came back to Hembree."

"And the child?"

"No idea. He or she probably doesn't know anything about it."

"I don't know." Carlotta slowly shook her head. "Adopted kids usually find out eventually."

"Well, that's all water under the bridge."

Carlotta sighed and raised her brow. "And Jack Eldridge—?"

"Well, I would imagine he knows he has a child in the world somewhere...other than his *legitimate* son Johnny."

"Hmm," Carlotta said, perturbed at Dot's choice of words. "Okay, I appreciate your telling me, and, don't worry, I won't tell a living soul." She gathered up the papers and stuffed them back in the folders. "These go back in as they were?"

"For the time being," Dot said. "I'll have to think what to do with them."

"Okay, you think," Carlotta said, "but in the meantime, leave all the files here. I may do some more rummaging. Never hurts to know who your clients are."

Chapter Twenty-Five

November 6, 2:30 p.m.
Frye, Frye, and Humphrey

Mosey waited till mid-afternoon to approach Frye, Frye, and Humphrey. A second visit in one week seemed out of character, given she had dropped in on Dot no more than three or four times in a year. But she was anxious to share her gossip—it was hardly more than that—with an expert on the subject of old Hembreeites. If anyone was privy to a connection between the affairs of Waite House and Sunny Banks, likely it was Dot. As to this most recent business, however, she had a feeling Carlotta might know even more.

She tapped lightly on the door as she turned the knob. "Good afternoon, Dot."

"Mosey Frye, I'm surprised to see you again so soon."

Surprised? Dot—before a file cabinet, lifting in files—didn't look surprised, not in a good way. Startled, maybe.

"Did you want to speak to Carlotta? She's gone over to the courthouse, but you know I'd love the company."

"No, you're busy."

"Not too busy to talk to you." She smiled nervously. "I'm just tidying up these cabinets, swapping some of these old folders for new ones, relabeling a few things."

She closed the cabinet and returned to her desk. "What can I do for you?"

"I wanted to talk with you about something—something I heard yesterday. Carlotta, too, but if she's not here…"

"She'll be back, but in the meantime, I'd be glad to listen." Her face brightened.

"I suppose I need to start at the beginning, or this isn't going to make any sense."

"Of course, but don't you want to have a seat, hon?"

"You know," she said, sitting at the end of the sofa closer to Dot, "I've sort of been involved in the sale of the Eldridge place."

"Yes, I think I knew that." Dot swiveled around and reached into her tote. "Can I get you something, Mosey," she said as she pulled out a bottle of water.

"No, thanks."

"As you were saying?" She took a sip.

"John Earle stopped by the office yesterday, mentioned that Mr. Eldridge Sr. was upset about the incident at Sunny Banks and wanted some reassurance from *us*—me, in other words. So, I went over to the Magnolia yesterday afternoon, just to cheer him up, let him know we were seeing after his property and there was no cause for alarm."

"That was nice of you. I'm sure he appreciated that."

"I don't believe I'd ever met him before. I was a little surprised. He's a handsome man, I mean, for his age, tall, broad shouldered, nicely dressed. And he didn't seem all that feeble. Every time the attendant tried to take his arm, he jerked it away."

"That's Martin for you. He's of my generation more or less. Always was a proud man. Old age is hard on men like him, the ones who've always been in charge. They don't like others coming in and taking over their lives. I can see why he'd be concerned about Sunny Banks."

"His car, too."

Dot shook her head. "What's done is done, and there's no changing it."

"I asked him if he had any idea why his property might have become the scene of this incident. He said he figured it had something to do with an *enemy from the past*, maybe a crew member who held a grudge, someone who'd been injured in a towboat accident. I asked him if he felt certain it was business related. At first he seemed to think so, and then he said that it might be something else, *but it was a long time ago*. He's been thinking about it, he said—this thing, whatever it was. 'Sometimes you make an enemy,' he said, 'and he never goes away. He never goes away, but never shows his ugly face, either.' I told him that if he knew something, he ought to tell Lieutenant Olivera. It was to his advantage to get this business resolved, so he could put it all behind him. And then he said he didn't expect that would ever happen."

"Oh, my, that does sound ominous. An enemy who never goes away but never shows his face. I wonder what on earth he meant."

"Well, I'm sure I don't know, but I wondered if maybe *you* knew or Carlotta." She shifted in her seat. She wanted to tell Dot what her daddy had said but couldn't think how to put it without letting Dot in on the secret.

"Mosey, sometimes these old quarrels are better left alone. Digging up the past can get you in a heap of trouble. You know what they say about letting sleeping dogs lie."

"That's true. But I'm afraid in this case, the past has

already come back to haunt us. The sleeping dog has woken up. A man's dead."

"I know, I know," she said with a deep sigh.

"You remember about a year ago," Mosey said, "when you and I were talking about Waite House and how Daddy used to tell me to stay away from there?"

"Uh-huh, I remember that conversation."

"You explained why you thought Daddy wouldn't want me going over there. It had something to do with Mona Waite and her sudden disappearance."

"Yes, that's right." Dot nodded. "I thought it might have something to do with that."

"I'm beginning to feel like this incident at Sunny Banks is somehow related to Waite House, but I can't for the life of me figure out what the connection is. If we knew that, I suspect we might know a lot." Mosey stood and moved toward the file cabinets. "These old files here, full of information about the Waites, the Eldridges. Too bad they can't talk among themselves. They might be able to figure this out."

Dot picked up a folder and started to fan herself.

"Are you okay?" Mosey said to Dot. "You look quite flushed."

"I'm feeling a little light-headed," Dot said. "I think I'll take one of my pills." She opened a side drawer and pulled out a medicine bottle.

"You want to lie down on the sofa?"

"No, no, I'll be fine." She popped the pill in her mouth and drank some water. "I get these little palpitations sometimes. They pass quickly. I'll be fine."

"Dot, I think maybe you need to go home. I'd be glad to run you home."

"It's not necessary."

"Well, at least let me call Carlotta."

"No, no, no, I don't want to bother her while she's at the courthouse. Let me just sit here a minute."

"Okay, but I'm staying with you, at least till Carlotta gets back."

Mosey convinced Dot to move to the sofa and prop her feet up. The two sat together quietly till Carlotta arrived a short time later.

"Mosey, hi," Carlotta said, coming in the door. "Dot…you okay?"

"She felt light-headed, and I didn't want to leave her till you got here."

"What happened?"

"Nothing," Dot said. "Just like Mosey said, I felt light-headed."

"Your a-fib acting up?" Carlotta asked.

"A-fib," Mosey said. "Dot, I didn't know you had a-fib."

"Oh, it's not a big deal."

"It can be," Carlotta said, "if you don't do what the doctor told you to."

"I try," Dot said.

"Mosey," Carlotta said, "why don't you come into my office. Let's let Dot rest. That's the best thing for her."

"Okay, if you say so." Mosey got up. "I offered to run her home, but she wouldn't hear of it."

"Come on in." Carlotta pushed back the door, but, before entering, turned to Dot. "You stay put, and if you need something holler."

Carlotta set her briefcase on her desk. "Now, then. Let's sit over here." She sat at the mahogany table.

Mosey took the chair next to hers. "I hope I didn't

say anything to upset Dot."

"Like what, for heaven's sake?"

"I wanted to talk to y'all about something Mr.
Eldridge said yesterday. I stopped by the nursing home,
just to let him know we were on top of things—the sale
of his property, I mean."

Carlotta's brow went up. "And?"

Mosey shifted in her seat. "He seemed to have his
mind on the property, but then it seemed like he was
more concerned about the crime itself—why it had
occurred at Sunny Banks."

"Go on."

"I think he was afraid of something. He said,
'Sometimes you make an enemy, and he never goes
away. Never goes away but never shows his ugly face,
either.' Dot said she thought it sounded ominous, and I
think so, too. I can't explain this, but I also think it's tied
in somehow with the Waites. You think the Waites and
the Eldridges had some kind of falling out?"

Carlotta leaned back. "All I can say about this is I'm
not at liberty to say."

"Oh, privileged information."

She nodded, her expression a bit sullen.

"Sorry," Mosey said. "I guess I should mind my own
business."

"Let's just say that I have similar concerns, and I'll
be looking into it."

"Well, that makes me feel better." She got up to
leave. "One more thing. I don't suppose there's any way
to share our suspicions with Lieutenant Olivera."

"I'm working on it."

She eyed Carlotta, who looked deep in thought. "I'd
better be running," she said. "Don't get up. I'll show

myself out."

Customarily, Carlotta would have seen her out, maybe given her a hug. But not this time. She continued to sit, swiveling and staring ahead. Mosey might have said "bye" again, but instead she slipped out quietly, pulling the door closed behind her.

Dot was still lying on the sofa, eyes shut. She didn't disturb her, just closed the outer door noiselessly and went on her way—indeed, more curious than when she had come. What in heaven's name had she stumbled into? With a "huh" and a shake of her head, she descended the stairs to the Square.

Chapter Twenty-Six

November 6, 8:00 a.m.
Hembree Police Station

Olivera arrived at the station earlier than usual. He was anxious to get back to his evidence board, figure out what data he could add after searching the victim's residence. He had documents to go through. What else? The car, yes. He wanted to put out an all-points bulletin on Ashby's car. "Springer," he called, raising his voice.

"Hold on a second, Chief."

A minute later, he came through the door, a cup of coffee in one hand, a donut in the other.

"Put an APB out on Ashby's car," Olivera said. "You got all the specs?"

"Sure do."

"You pick up any prints yesterday at the house?"

"Quite a few, but nothing that didn't match the victim's."

"Anything else of interest?"

"Paper stuff—bills, documents, that sort of thing."

"We'll need to go through all that, but put out the APB first. If we can find the car, it might lead us to the crime scene, to the perpetrator, even."

"We still don't know if it's a homicide, right, Chief?"

"That's right."

"What are we waiting on?" He sounded disgruntled.

"Cause of death," Olivera said.

Springer raised his brows but said nothing. "I'll put out the APB. Anything else?"

"Yeah, bring me some coffee and one of those donuts."

"What kind you want? We got chocolate, glazed, blueberry—"

"Surprise me."

Springer left, and Olivera wrote the make and model of Ashby's car on a tab and pinned it to the board below the post-mortem photographs. Leaning back, he folded his arms across his chest and muttered under his breath, "Such a paltry bit of information on the victim..." It was as if Ashby didn't want his identity known. Could that be a possibility? Had he come to Hembree on some kind of secret mission? Something that kept him from forming relationships? Or maybe he was running from the law. Doubtful. Surely, Blanchard had given him a thorough going over before hiring him. He picked up the phone and punched in the number of Personnel at the college. "Lieutenant Olivera here. I wonder if you could tell me something concerning hiring protocols."

"Let me let you speak with Ms. Herman."

"Fine."

A few bars of the alma mater played, and Olivera sang along. "Alma mater, dear old—"

"Hello, Lieutenant."

"Ms. Herman," he said, clearing his throat. "Uh, I have a question about your hiring protocol."

"Sure. What specifically did you want to know?"

"When you hire an administrator, how thorough a check do you do?—into his background, I mean."

"Not that thorough, I'm afraid. We look mostly at academic records. We depend on recommendations to alert us to problems. What makes you ask?"

"What we've been able to gather on Charles Ashby is rather thin. You suppose, if he'd had anything unusual in his background, it would've come out?"

"If you're asking me if we do a search for criminal records, no. However, an academic record—transcripts, diplomas, and all—would likely alert us to anything, well—"

"Okay, thanks. By the way, Ashby had a car, but it's not in his garage. I was thinking it might be on campus. Would you mind checking with your Parking and Transit?"

"Certainly," she said. "I'll do that right away. It may take half an hour or so for campus police to do a search."

"No problem. Let me know when you hear back."

Springer came in, set a mug and a cinnamon donut wrapped in a napkin on the desk.

"Thanks, Springer," he said as he reached for the mug. "The documents are in the evidence room?"

"They are."

"And by the way, did you get a match on the fingerprints on the steering wheel?"

"I thought I told you that, Chief. The steering wheel was wiped clean. Not a print on it."

"Interesting." Olivera sipped his coffee. "You know, this is looking more and more like a homicide."

"If you ask me, it's looked like a homicide from the get-go."

"Yeah, I guess it has." He got up. "If anybody wants me, I'll be in the evidence room."

At the evidence room door, Olivera pulled his key

out of his pocket, then saw the door was open. "Springer, the door's unlocked again."

"Sorry, Chief."

"Try to remember, would you?" He shook his head and, going into the room, flipped on the light. He meandered his way through boxes and sundry items to the back wall, where Springer had left the utility cart with the evidence. There was little there, other than some of the bottles from the cabin and the box of documents from the victim's residence. The blood samples, fibers, and the computer registered to Martin Eldridge were already at the morgue. He picked up the box, and, balancing it on his hip, locked the door and headed back to his office. Surely there would be something in the man's personal papers that could point him in the right direction. He entered his cubicle and, setting the donut to one side, put the box down and settled into his chair. "Okay," he mumbled, "for the umpteenth time, who the devil are you, Charles Duncan Ashby?" He thumbed through the folders, reading labels as he went. "Water, hmm. Light. Gas." Pushing the stack aside, he droned, "At least you were organized."

Having found nothing of interest among the small folders, he moved on to one of several envelope folders and, untying the ribbon, pulled out the operating manual for a vacuum cleaner. "Give me a break, would you? How many bleeping manuals can one man have?" He tossed it aside and went on to the next and the next. The contents of the other folders were similar—manuals, warranties, insurance policies, all ordered by kind and date, all neatly tucked into envelopes. "So what have we here—a cable bill? A subscription to *GQ*?" he said mockingly, untying a folder neither labeled nor dated and flatter than the rest. He shook it, and a manila envelope fell out. Addressed to Ashby, it contained several sheets held together with a clip. Across the top was printed, "James Henry, Private Detective." The perfunctory letter, which began, "Dear Mr. Ashby," informed the addressee of the completion of Henry's report as well as his acknowledgment of payment in full for services rendered. "Hmm," Olivera muttered as he came to the total cost of Henry's services. "That's a hefty price to pay. Must have been important."

The first page of the document gave the background information of the subject, Martin. J. Eldridge III...aka Johnny Eldridge. The report itself began on the second page and was typed on a template similar to others he had seen. Company, investigator's name, beginning date of investigation, completed on, and score. He flipped to the next page and perused the evidence and conclusion—" 'Clear evidence proves that the subject attempted to extort money...' " He paused and skimmed the statement until he came to the last paragraph. " 'Therefore,' " he read, " 'the allegations are substantiated.' " He tapped the desk with his knuckles. "We already knew that, didn't we?" He continued on to the complaint summary. " 'On June 1, an anonymous tip was received through the Eldridge and Son Employee Hotline, accusing Martin J. Eldridge III (aka Johnny Eldridge) of having attempted to extort money from crew members of the *Captain Jack*. The source claimed he had received an email threatening to reveal his involvement in the crash of the tugboat on April 15. According to the source, some of the other crew members received similar threats.' Wow...just wow." He picked up the donut, took a bite, and chewed.

The next few pages, labeled "Evidence," contained interviews conducted with the crew members who had received blackmail messages. They all denied having consumed alcohol on the night in question.

Olivera took another bite of the donut. "Springer." He wiped his mouth with the napkin.

"Yeah, Chief?"

Olivera held up the report. "You see this?"

Springer nodded.

"This is the clincher."

"What is it?" Springer's eyes grew big.

"You know who James Henry is?"

"Why, yeah, he's a PI—"

"—hired by Ashby to investigate Martin J. 'Johnny' Eldridge."

"The hideout guy?"

"The hideout guy, whose computer contained the blackmail messages referred to in this report."

"So, Ashby hired Henry to investigate Eldridge, and Eldridge hauled off and killed him, or had him killed—whatever."

Olivera smiled. "I'd say we've got motive. Call Judge Hendricks's clerk and tell her we're going to need an arrest warrant for Martin J. Eldridge III. But get Eldridge's contact information before you call. I'll provide the details when I get there."

Olivera picked up a tab and printed "suspects," and then, on another tab, "Johnny Eldridge." He sat back to scrutinize the evidence. There was one thing he didn't quite get—actually, didn't get at all—how a relative newcomer to Hembree became privy to an extortion scheme. He had no thoughts on the subject, but he bet he knew who did. Carlotta Humphrey, whose family had lawyered for the Eldridges from way back. Getting her to open up on a client wouldn't be easy but definitely worth a try. He pinned the tabs to the board. If he could convince Carlotta that Johnny had committed a crime, she might soften up, especially if she thought spilling the beans on Johnny might in the end protect the company and the family. He shook his head. "Touch and go."

Olivera stared out the window, remembering a conversation that he'd had with Carlotta during his investigation of Ninon Bilyeu's murder. She'd readily delivered up the contents of the victim's will. But, of course, Carlotta's loyalty apparently lay with Ninon more than with the other members of the Bilyeu clan. Again, they were dealing with multiple family members. Would Carlotta side with old Martin and son Jack? Johnny, after all, had turned on the *Captain Jack* crew and, ultimately, the company. Unless, of course, Jack had put him up to it. No. He shook his head. He didn't believe that. Nothing he'd learned so far had pointed the finger at Jack. Johnny was the rogue, Jack, the good guy. And he imagined Carlotta knew that.

Chapter Twenty-Seven

November 6, 2:00 p.m.
Morgue, Delta Infirmary

Tengo la cabeza como un bombo. Of course, Olivera was exaggerating. His orderly mind wasn't at all like a garbage can. But today, with the case developing more quickly than he liked, he was feeling a bit overwrought. He stood at the entrance to the morgue, glancing around at cracked plaster, which had weathered the passing of time more poorly than the terrazzo tile beneath his feet.

On occasions such as this, McGinnis had become his go-to person, his guru of sorts. She was younger than he, less experienced, and yet he had come to revere her methodical approach to things. He pressed his shoulder against the heavy door and pushed. "Dr. McGinnis, glad you're here."

"Where else?" She was sitting at her desk toward the back of the room.

"Well, it's Friday, and I'd gladly take you for a drink this afternoon if—"

"You don't have to bribe me, Lieutenant." She chuckled. "What's up?"

"I wasn't trying to bribe you." He removed his hat. "But we'll get to that later. What I really want is to bring you up to date on a couple of things." He passed the empty autopsy table on his way to her desk, pausing to give it a tap. "You know, of course, we've identified the victim. Charles Duncan Ashby is his name. He worked at the Development Office at Blanchard. We searched his house yesterday—it's a few blocks off the Square— and we found some documents that have been helpful, *very* helpful." He sat and propped an elbow on her desk. "Get this. Ashby had Johnny Eldridge investigated. I found the PI report in a box of papers."

"Our Johnny, Johnny of the computer?"

He nodded. "And guess what for."

"Extortion."

He cocked his head. "You're good."

She smiled then scrunched her forehead. "What tipped him off? I mean—"

"I know," he cut in. "My thoughts exactly. Ashby arrived in Hembree a little over a year ago, so how'd he happen to come across *this*? How did he know anything about Johnny Eldridge's attempt to extort money from the crew?"

"Hmm. We already knew—" She paused. "—or at least suspected there was some connection between Ashby and the Eldridges. The body was found on Eldridge property. The car belonged to Johnny's grandfather. Then there was the hair from two different people, *similar* hair." She tilted her head toward the autopsy table, although the body wasn't there. "If only we had the DNA results."

"No word on that yet?"

"No, and I have a mind to call them again. If we had the results, we'd know if the unknown hair was Johnny's."

"And without it, my only option is to arrest him on suspicion of blackmail. Of course, the PI report speaks to motive."

"If Ashby learned about Johnny's scheme and was about to bring him down, Johnny would have wanted him out of the way." Her eyes narrowed. "My question is how did Ashby find out."

"According to the PI report, a crew member reported it on the employee hotline."

She frowned. "But how would Ashby have access to that?"

"Somebody who worked for the company must have told him."

"I guess. But who?"

"What keeps coming up for me is *why*? This unexplained interest—" He broke off mid-sentence. "I'm baffled."

"And yet, I think we've both had a hunch from the beginning that there *is* a connection."

"I'm not especially anxious to do this," he said, "but I think I'm going to have to speak to Carlotta Humphrey again. She's their lawyer. Maybe she knows something or, if she doesn't, maybe she would be willing to take a look at her files."

"You think she might know something about Ashby?"

"When I talked to her about the sale of the property, she didn't seem to. She didn't recognize him from the post-mortem pictures. But knowing what I know now, that Johnny was attempting to blackmail company employees and that Ashby knew... Well, at the very least, she'll want to know that. I'm not sure what her role might be if Johnny is brought up on charges."

"You suppose Johnny would hire her to defend him?"

"Maybe." He shrugged. "She's the family lawyer."

"I think you should speak to her."

"I'm headed in that direction now. I've got to pick up an arrest warrant at the courthouse. And listen—" He picked up his hat. "—suppose I drop by around six. Will you still be here?"

"No doubt."

"Would you like to grab a drink at the Tavernette— or we can go somewhere else if you prefer?"

"The Tavernette sounds fine."

He smiled. "Good, I'll be back."

Chapter Twenty-Eight

November 6, 3:00 p.m.
Frye, Frye, and Humphrey

As Olivera was ascending the stairs, Mosey Frye was coming down.

"Ms. Frye." He tipped his hat.

"Lieutenant," she said with a smile, "just the person I wanted to see."

"Actually, I'm in a bit of rush."

"This won't take a second, I promise. It's about the case. Mr. Eldridge, Martin Eldridge Sr., is kind of upset about a body being found on his property. At least that's what I thought before I went over there, to the Magnolia. But after we talked, seemed like he knew something, something related to the incident. I told him he ought to get in touch with you, but I somehow doubt he will."

"Hmm," he whirred, drumming his fingers on the hand rail. "So, he's unlikely to get in touch, you think."

"Yeah, I don't see it happening, but maybe *you* should get in touch with *him*."

"I suppose I could."

"And one more thing, Lieutenant. You have any idea when the case might be resolved? Two of my clients, one on one side, one on the other, are mighty anxious to know."

"Side of what?"

"One buyer—"

"Oh, Lauren Wilson, you mean."

"Yes, and Mr. Eldridge. Looks like Shepherd Realty will represent the seller and the buyer."

"I can't say for sure," he said, "but we're moving forward, yes, definitely moving forward."

"That's hopeful. I'll tell them that."

"Okay, well, thanks for that information." He tipped his hat again.

"You're welcome."

He got to the top of the stairs and pressed the doorbell.

"Go on in," Mosey called up to him. "Dot's lying down."

He frowned, removed his hat, and opened the door. "Ms. Cowsley?" He turned toward Dot, who was stretched out on the sofa. "Are you okay?"

She raised her head and waved at him with a handkerchief. "Lieutenant Olivera," she said weakly, "were we expecting you this afternoon?"

"No, ma'am. I thought I might catch Ms. Humphrey in." He closed the door behind him. "Is she here?"

"She is. Let me see if she's free." Dot sat up. "Oh, my. I'm still a little light-headed."

"Why don't you stay where you are, and I'll knock on the door."

"No, Lieutenant, that wouldn't do, wouldn't do at all. You have a seat, and I'll give Carlotta a buzz." She got to her feet and, holding onto the desk, inched toward her chair. She picked up the receiver. "Carlotta, Lieutenant Olivera is here. He'd like to speak to you if you're free." She nodded to Olivera, motioning for him to go in.

He knocked lightly on the door.

"Come in, Lieutenant."

"Thanks for seeing me," he said.

"Not at all. Actually, this is a timely visit."

"It is?"

"Yes—" She waved an arm toward the upholstered chairs. "—but I'm not sure where to start. Have a seat."

She wasn't sure where to start. That came as a surprise, which, after knowing Carlotta for a year, was no surprise at all. She was the most alluringly inscrutable individual he'd ever come across. He'd never seen her in the courtroom but thought it must be a sight to behold. Not knowing where to start, either—though he'd had a plan of sorts—he simply repeated her words in the form of a question. "You aren't sure where to start?" He stood by the mahogany table, waiting for her to sit.

She moved toward the closest chair, bringing a file with her. "Yeah, I really don't know—"

"Start anywhere," he said.

"Might as well." She sat and placed the file on the table.

He sat, too, craning his neck to read the label on the file. But, upside down, he couldn't tell what it said.

"You and I both, Lieutenant, are standing near a past, let's say, about which neither of us knows very much, if anything."

He said nothing, just knitted his brow.

"And now something has occurred that begs for clarification. Most the people concerned—who *were* concerned—have either passed on or left Hembree, and the person *most* concerned doesn't seem to have a clue."

He leaned in. "I'm sorry, but I'm not quite following you."

"Of course you aren't. How could you? I can offer you a piece of the puzzle, but I can't connect the dots, and I'm not sure who can."

"A piece of the puzzle would be good," he said.

"Okay, this is what I know," she said, lightly tapping the file. "But it must remain vague. I *can't* tell you all I know, but I can tell you this. I have a client who has a child he doesn't know is his."

"A child he doesn't know is his." What in blazes did *that* have to do with anything? He shifted in his seat and calmly asked, "And could you tell me how old that child might be?"

"I can tell you almost exactly how old he or she is. He's, let's see..." She picked up a pad and scribbled some numbers. "Thirty-nine."

"Ha, Jack Benny's age."

She grinned.

"That's the second thirty-nine-year-old I've run across this week," he said. "Charles Ashby was thirty-nine."

She nodded.

"I don't suppose you could tell me if Ashby and this child...well, let me start again...if Ashby *is* this child."

She shook her head. "I can't tell you that."

"Okay, well, maybe I can do something with that." He cleared his throat. "Actually, I have some information I thought you'd want to know. We searched Ashby's house yesterday and came across a report from a private investigator. Ashby hired James Henry—maybe you've heard of him—to look into a possible crime." He scooted toward the front of his chair. "Ashby suspected Johnny Eldridge of extortion, and the evidence the PI presented in his report suggests Ashby's suspicions were well founded. Seems Eldridge tried to blackmail some crew members in connection with the April 15 crash of the *Captain Jack*. I'm sure you know about the accident."

"Yes, of course." She took a deep breath. "And I suppose I will be reading about this in the paper?"

"Afraid so," he said.

"Do you have a warrant for Johnny's arrest?"

"I'll have to remain vague about that," he said, "for the time being."

Carlotta stood and returned to her desk.

He stood as well and, as he left her office, glimpsed furtively at the file she'd left on the table. "Family Lines," the label read. Huh.

On his way out, he checked on Dot, who was standing over an open file cabinet. "I hope you're feeling better, Ms. Cowsley."

"I'm fine, Lieutenant. You have a nice day."

He smiled and waved his hat as he left.

So what in heaven's name was *that* all about? Charles Ashby was thirty-nine. One of her clients had an unknown thirty-nine-year-old son or daughter. Was the file a clue? Family Lines…Eldridge and Son Barge Lines. Was she suggesting the unenlightened father was Jack Eldridge? He took the stairs two by two and, upon reaching the sidewalk, paused. "Wouldn't *that* take the cake?" He pulled out his phone and made a call. A soft voice answered, one he liked to hear. "Dr. McGinnis, Olivera here."

"Yes, Lieutenant."

"A peculiar piece of information has fallen into my lap. Might we seriously put a rush on the DNA?"

"I've already called, and they say they'll do what they can."

"I strongly suspect that when we have it—" He broke off, thinking he needed to think some more before laying it all out before McGinnis.

"Yes?"

"Never mind. I'll tell you when I pick you up. Six, we said?"

"Sure, Lieutenant, see you then."

Chapter Twenty-Nine

November 6, 4:00 p.m.
County Courthouse, Hembree

Waiting outside Judge Hendricks's chambers, Olivera sat staring into space till the tall wooden door opened and the clerk stepped out. "Here you go, Lieutenant," she said as she handed him the warrant. Then peering over the top of berry-colored half rims, she said, "If I were you, I'd check on his whereabouts before I tried to serve this."

"Why's that?" he asked. Did she know something about Johnny Eldridge that he didn't?

"He works on the river. He could be anywhere." She shrugged.

"Oh, right," he said. "And who would know?"

"I'd call the barge lines."

"Thank you, I'll do that."

She turned and re-entered the chamber.

Outside the building, he called Eldridge and Son and got the receptionist. "This is Lieutenant Olivera of the Hembree Police Department. I need to get in touch with Johnny Eldridge."

"Mr. Eldridge is on the *Sara Katherine*."

"And where is the *Sara Katherine*?"

"Downriver about thirty miles from here. You just missed him. He was here this morning."

"When do you expect him back?" he said.

"About ten days."

"Okay, thank you."

That was a setback. But he wasn't waiting any ten days to serve the warrant. He'd have to call the Coast Guard. He propped himself against the side of the building and made the call. "Lieutenant Gustavo Olivera here, of the Hembree Police Department. I have a warrant for the arrest of Johnny Eldridge, that's Martin J. Eldridge III, and I was wondering if you could help me out. He's on a towboat, the *Sara Katherine*, downriver about thirty miles from Vicksburg."

"What's the warrant for?" the officer asked.

"Extortion, but he's also wanted for questioning in a possible homicide."

"I see. Okay, fax us the warrant, and we'll pick him up. Do you have our fax number?"

"We must have it at the office," Olivera said. "One more thing, Officer. If you could deliver him to Lake Village, we could run down and pick him up."

"I'll have to check on that. I'll let you know."

Olivera called Springer. "Springer, I've got the arrest warrant, but turns out Johnny Eldridge is on a towboat thirty miles downriver from Vicksburg and won't be back for ten days."

"What you gonna do, Chief?"

"I've already called the Coast Guard. They'll pick him up."

"Did you tell them he's a suspect in a homicide?"

"I did. Check on something for me, Springer. Make sure we've got the fax number for the Coast Guard. I'll be there in a few minutes. We need to fax them the warrant."

"Okay, but I'm pretty sure we do."

"I'm on the Square. See you in a minute."

He reached the office, and Springer was waiting, ready to fax the warrant. "I guess there's nothing to do now but wait," Olivera said.

"Oh, I imagine they'll get him here pretty quick. If he's thirty miles from Vicksburg, that's no piece. You reckon they'll send a boat for him?"

"Sure, what else?" Olivera asked.

"I've known 'em to send a helicopter."

"I doubt that happens. Hold on. I just got a text from the Coast Guard. We can pick him up in Lake Village."

"Squad car's ready to go, Chief, when you are."

"I thought I might send you and Reagan. Think you can handle it?"

"Well, of course, we can. You can trust us."

"So, you and Reagan take care of that. I've got some loose ends to tie up."

The first loose end concerned the information he'd learned from Mosey Frye. He hadn't figured on speaking with the eldest Eldridge, but after she'd said what she had, he thought he'd better follow up. Not everything she suggested made sense, but this did. Why hadn't he thought of it himself?

He got to the station and, passing by reception, spoke to Ms. Hill. "Would you get the Magnolia Nursing Home on the phone? Tell them to expect me. I'd like to speak to one of their residents, Mr. Martin Eldridge."

Ms. Hill made the call, then held the receiver to her chest. "They want to know when to expect you."

He checked his watch. "Let's say in quarter of an hour."

"He'll be there in fifteen minutes." She nodded, and

Olivera, hat in hand, went on his way.

Once at the nursing home, he spoke with the receptionist. "Lieutenant Olivera here to see Mr. Martin Eldridge?" He'd phrased it as a question. Somehow it seemed more polite. And politeness went a long way in Hembree. "Ms. Hill just spoke with you?"

Despite his mannerly approach, the receptionist gave him exactly the look he'd expected, as if she were a momma cat and he was about to pick up one of her kittens. "Have a seat over there if you want." She threw a thumb in the general direction of the sun parlor, then walked from behind the counter and down the dimly-lit hall.

Olivera sat on a wicker settee. It was his first visit to the Magnolia, and he glanced around, expecting more hustle and bustle. There was no one around. The room was silent. He picked up a copy of the *Hembree Shopper* and paged through, till he heard the approach of shuffling feet. He laid the *Shopper* on the cushion next to his. An elderly man, in the company of the receptionist, had emerged from the hall. Olivera rose.

"Don't keep him too long," the receptionist said. "He's got his supper in half an hour."

He greeted the tall gentleman at her side. "Mr. Eldridge?"

"That's right. Who'd you expect?" He waggled his head.

"Well, you, of course. I'm Lieutenant Olivera of the Hembree Police. Might we speak for a moment?"

Eldridge eased into a straight chair next to a small glass-top table. "Getting up and down isn't so easy as it used to be." He rested his arm on the table.

"Mr. Eldridge," he began, "it's my understanding

that you're concerned about the recent incident involving your property."

"Indeed, I am, sir. Wouldn't you be?"

"I imagine I would." He sat across from Eldridge.

"How long are you going to keep my car?"

"I expect we'll be able to release it soon."

"And what about my house? I suppose this *incident*, as you called it, has thrown a monkey wrench into that, too."

"If I had to guess, within the month, two at the most."

"And this fellow who was killed—" He lifted his chin. "—what was his name?"

"Charles Ashby."

"You don't know what he was doing at Sunny Banks, do you?" Eldridge asked.

"I expect I may know before long."

"How's that?"

"We have—or are soon to have—a suspect in custody."

Eldridge leaned forward. "You mean you've arrested somebody?"

"We're in the process—"

"It's not my grandson, is it?" Eldridge cut in.

Startled at his question, Olivera stammered, "What, uh, would make you think that?"

"I tell you what." Eldridge pointed his index finger straight at him and, squinting, said, "You answer my question. Then I'll answer yours."

"Okay. Well…yes…we do have him on our suspect list." Olivera rubbed his fingers in front of his mouth. He wasn't being completely truthful and knew it, but it seemed like the kinder thing to say.

"I thought so," Eldridge said with a frown. "Johnny got in an argument with that fellow Ashby."

"Go on."

"He told me all about it. Ashby was snooping around, prying into Johnny's affairs."

"And why was that?"

"I don't know, but I have my suspicions."

"Did you know Charles Ashby?"

"No, but I think I know who he is—was." He raised a trembling hand to his forehead. "I saw his picture in the paper, and I have a hunch. I..." He shook his head. "I think he might be my grandson."

"You saw his picture, and you think you recognized him as your grandson?" Olivera sat forward, thinking he was about to get another piece of the puzzle. Carlotta had given him one, and now it sounded like Eldridge was giving him another. He remained silent, not wanting to jinx his run of luck. And more than that, he was starting to feel sad for the old guy and wanted to make it easier for him if he could.

Eldridge, who'd been staring down at the table top, looked up. Swollen and red, his faded blue eyes were filling up with tears. He took out a handkerchief and daubed at his face. "My son had a child. He and Mona Waite had a baby. That happened thirty-nine years ago. Thirty-nine years...when Jack was just twenty. We never saw the child, never knew if it was a boy or a girl. But when I saw that picture and saw his age, I had a hunch that man was my grandson, and I've never laid eyes on him."

He waited a moment out of respect for Eldridge's revelation. "Did you share this hunch with anyone, sir, your son Jack or his son Johnny?"

"I told Jack. He said he'd look into it." He shook his head. "Too many coincidences, Lieutenant. Too many coincidences."

Olivera for the second time that day was at a loss for words. He needed to think about it all, all the parts to the improbable conundrum. He looked at his watch. It was close to five. He had a date with McGinnis at six. "Mr. Eldridge, I'm terribly sorry—" He was about to say *for your loss*, but then it struck him that they didn't know for sure if Charles Ashby *was* his grandson, just as they didn't know for sure if Johnny Eldridge, his half-brother, maybe, had killed him. The pieces seemed to be fitting together that way, but he wasn't going to rule out other possibilities until something concrete suggested he should.

Eldridge told him he'd like to be alone, and Olivera offered to help him back to his room. But Eldridge said he thought he'd sit in the parlor a spell, enjoy the last rays of the afternoon sun. Olivera shook the man's hand and left.

Chapter Thirty

Friday, November 6, 8 p.m.
County Lock-up

Olivera picked up McGinnis at the morgue and drove to the Tavernette in time to catch the end of happy hour. But hoping their time together might be a leisurely end to a long week, he was annoyed at his failure to disentangle himself from the case at hand. He kept checking his cellphone, expecting a message from Springer. It came at last. Eldridge was in custody. So, after dropping McGinnis off at her home, he headed over to the local lock-up, where an officer escorted him to the suspect's cell.

Surprisingly, Eldridge hadn't yet lawyered up. Nor did he seem particularly rattled—another surprise. He just sat there, leaning against the cinder block wall, hands tucked under his arms.

Olivera introduced himself, pulled up a chair, and, getting out his tablet and pencil, listened as Eldridge told his story. As he spoke, Olivera couldn't help but compare him with the other Eldridges, even Ashby. Johnny's dominant feature was his eyes, translucent blue like his father's, though, whereas in the father they expressed composure, in the son they conveyed something else, annoyance or a kind of brooding introspection. Hard to tell.

"Ashby got in touch with me," Eldridge began, "about buying my granddaddy's car, and I agreed to meet him at Sunny Banks as soon as I got off the boat. I'd left my car in Memphis, so I got one of the crew to drop me off at the house. It was a little late when I arrived, and Ashby was already there, checking out the Tyche—it was in the garage. He seemed eager to take it for a spin, so I gave him the key, and he took off. No—" He shook his head. "—that's not exactly right. I asked him for his driver's license first, just so I'd have something in case he decided not to come back."

"Did you have any reason to suspect he wouldn't?" Olivera asked.

"Not really," he said with a shrug, "but it just seemed like the right thing to do. I didn't really know the guy. I'd seen him a couple of times at the Tavernette, and that was about it."

"Okay, so then?"

"He sort of smirked, pulled his license, out of his wallet and left. He was gone about fifteen, twenty minutes. The house was locked, and I didn't have the key, so, I sat on the front porch and waited. When he pulled back in the drive, I walked over to the garage. He got out but didn't close the door, left it standing wide open, which seemed a little odd. Then he said to me, kind of cocky like, *he was going to get right back in and drive away*. Said he had a right to it—the car, the house, the business… That's when the argument began. I sort of backed away and headed toward the porch, where I'd left the license. I wouldn't have sold him the car, not after that, but he followed me, kept dangling the key in my face. I grabbed for it. He jerked it away, and, just as I got to the porch, he yelled something and I turned around.

He said he was my brother, half-brother, whatever, and he was going to get what was his."

"Was that the first you'd heard of that—that you might be related?"

He blinked, then squinted, as if he were reliving the moment of Ashby's bizarre revelation. "Of course," he stammered, "if I'd had any idea…"

"Did you speak to your father or grandfather, later on…after the accident?"

"Not right away, but, yeah, I asked 'em if they knew Charles Ashby. They said they didn't."

"Did you tell them anything else?"

"No." He shook his head, then got up, and paced toward the end of the cell.

"How did you react when Ashby told you he was your brother?"

He turned around and faced Olivera. "I said he was lying. I told him to get off the property. That's when he took a swing at me."

"So, you didn't take a swing at *him*? Didn't push him?"

"No, I never touched him. I ducked and he lost his balance. That's when he fell, hit his head on a big pot next to the door. He didn't get up. I thought he'd passed out. I listened to see if he was breathing. He wasn't. I couldn't think what to do except try CPR."

"Why didn't you call 911?" Olivera cut in.

"I should have." He came back to the cot and sat down. "But he was gone. I tried to get a pulse and couldn't. He was dead." He dropped his head, looked down at the floor. "I've been in fights before, but nothing like that. I didn't know what to do. It was pitch dark by then, and nobody was around, just me and…"

"Charles Ashby."

He nodded.

"You must have cleaned up before you left."

He nodded. "Yeah, the hose was right there in the garage, and after I closed the car door…"

"One more thing," Olivera cut in, "the body was found with no identification."

"I was going to put his driver's license back in his wallet, but when I reached in his pocket, I realized the license had my prints on it. I guess I was thinking like I was guilty."

"Well," Olivera said, "maybe you didn't kill him but *you are guilty*…of not reporting a death."

He looked up.

"That could get you one to five." Olivera got up and paced. "So finish your story. You were saying something about the garage."

"I was pretty anxious to get out of there, but before I left, I wiped down the Tyche and hosed off the garage floor and the porch. Then I took off in Charles's car. I left it in a parking lot off the Square and walked the rest of the way home."

"Did you go back over there—to the house I mean?"

He shook his head.

"So, if Mosey Frye hadn't discovered the body…"

"I don't know." He shook his head again. "I don't know what I would have done. I wanted to report it, but I knew how it'd look." He looked Olivera straight in the eye. "It happened just like I said. I never even touched him. I *did not* push him. If he hadn't fallen…"

As soon as Olivera left, he called Springer, and despite the late hour, the two of them drove out to Sunny Banks, where they discovered small traces of blood on the urn by the door. McGinnis had been wise in exerting caution regarding cause of death. The lip of the urn matched the shape of the wound on the back of Ashby's head.

Chapter Thirty-One

Saturday, November 14, 9:00 a.m.
Olivera's Home

Olivera sauntered back and forth between the breakfast table and the island, pausing at random to give Grim Milly Grimalkin a scratch behind the ears. He scooped her up and plopped her down on the counter. "You know something, girl?"

Rationality would have it that Grim Milly knew little beyond the common knowledge of a Russian Blue, though her eyes, vibrant and deep, bore a distinctive glint of intelligence.

"At the beginning of this—and I'm referring to the mysterious death of Charles Ashby—"

"Rrrow," she piped.

"It's okay, you didn't know him."

Comforted, evidently, by his tone if not his words, she began to purr.

He scratched under her chin and continued. "At first, I was especially curious to know why Ashby, a newcomer to Hembree, had taken an unequivocal interest in the Eldridge family, Johnny in particular. I was convinced it was no coincidence, and after my interview with Martin Sr., things began to fall into place. Follow me so far?" He rubbed his finger under her chin.

Milly stared back but didn't make a sound.

"I suppose it's hard to think on an empty stomach." He opened the refrigerator and pulled out a can of cat food, then scraped a large helping into her bowl. "Here you go."

"Rrrow."

"Okay, so Ashby, the dead man, must have discovered that Jack was his biological father. Maybe he submitted his DNA to a genetic testing company, or maybe whoever raised him told him about his birth parents—who knows?" He returned to the refrigerator and pulled out a carton of eggs and a bundle of flour tortillas wrapped in a tea towel. "But never mind how he came by the information, he must have decided to act on it. You see, Milly"—whose full attention he held by means of the occasional caress—"Ashby must have been an overly cautious person, like me, and, having misgivings about revealing his identity to strangers, decided to find out who they were—who they really were—before rushing into anything."

Olivera scrambled a couple of eggs, piled them onto a toasty tortilla, and rolled it into a burrito. "Yum, want a bite?"

Busily eating, Milly ignored his offer.

He poured himself a cup of tea and sat down at the table to eat his burrito and reconsider the events of the preceding week. Absent a human interlocutor, he laid it all out for Milly, his audience of one. Once he'd finished his account, he said, "Milly, it all fits, fits together nicely, wouldn't you say?"

She stopped licking her paw and glanced in his direction before continuing her cleaning ritual.

"But why, then—" He took a sip of his tea. "—am I sitting here on a delightful Saturday morning, talking to you, letting my burrito get cold—" He paused to take a bite. "—ruminating over the facts of the case?"

Indeed, a full week had passed since Eldridge's arrest, and, during that week—*milagro de milagros*—Olivera had managed to close the case. But despite having closed it, to his way of thinking, there was still work to be done. Nothing official, mind you, but there was *something* he needed to know concerning the victim's character. Eldridge had seen a side of Ashby that the others had not. To Johnny, he was a man hell-bent on taking what belonged to him: the car, the house, *even the company*, for crying out loud.

After Olivera had eaten the last bite of burrito, he poured himself a second cup of tea and went back to the bedroom. Setting the cup on the dresser, he reached into the top drawer for a t-shirt and joggers. "And another thing…a pretty *big* thing." He turned to Milly, who'd followed him into the bedroom. "Johnny swore—I learned this from Carlotta—he hadn't had anything to do with the blackmail scheme. That certainly came as a surprise. He said it was a frame up, a plot on Ashby's part to get him out of the way. He said he felt sure, though he had no proof, that Ashby had hacked his email and the company's employee hotline. *He*, Johnny, hadn't tried to buy off the crew—he had no reason to. As far as he knew, none of the men on the *Captain Jack* had been drinking the night of the crash. Bad weather, poor visibility had caused the accident, not management or the crew." Olivera put on his jogging gear and sat on the bed. "Johnny claimed," he said, pulling on a sock, "that his laptop had been stolen months before. He bought a replacement—had the receipt to prove it." He put on the other sock and his running shoes. "When I questioned him later, I told him about finding the laptop registered to Martin Eldridge in the hovel. He said he hadn't been anywhere near the hovel since he was in high school. Which made me wonder if Ashby hadn't discovered the hovel and used it to carry out his plot against Johnny— if there was a plot." He paused to tie his shoes. "But you know what, Milly? That explains the lack of prints on the computer. Ashby must have wiped it down, yeah, then left it in the hovel, thinking somebody might find it. The computer was a plant—must have been—and it worked."

He washed the breakfast dishes, slipped his house key into his pants pocket, and headed not to the Square, his habitual route, but to the college, where there was a track that circled the football field.

The cool air was exhilarating, and there was little traffic to slow him down. It hadn't been his intention to visit the victim's old stomping grounds, yet, when he came to the campus, he found himself slowing down in front of Founders Hall. He glanced at the bottom floor windows. Charles Ashby had once sat on the other side of those windows, conversing with his colleagues, planning promotional events. If he'd only left well enough alone, he might have had a nice career at the college, made Director of Development or President, *¿cómo no?* His colleagues thought him amicable, clever. But the question was…had he been clever enough to pull off all Johnny Eldridge said he had? Clever enough to cover his tracks? Might there be evidence either at the hovel or on the computer of a plot to bring Johnny down?

Olivera gave a mental shrug, and getting to the track, picked up speed and simultaneously pushed the case out of his mind. He ran a few laps, and as he headed home at a slow jog, he finished sorting through the last step, i. e., the trial, which hadn't taken place yet and most likely would not. The case would settle out of court, he imagined, given that murder charges would not be brought. The prosecutor would ask for a year for failure to report, but Olivera doubted Johnny would serve even that. Given his family's standing in the community…he might get a suspended sentence. He had no previous record…yep, probation is all he'd probably get.

The *Captain Jack* disaster had occurred in another jurisdiction, and Johnny and his lawyers—Carlotta among them—would have to put that matter to rest. He suspected that, once all was said and done, Johnny would be cleared of any wrongdoing. But he did intend, if only to satisfy his own curiosity, to follow up on the matter of Ashby's alleged set-up.

Chapter Thirty-Two

Monday, November 16, 9:00 a.m.
Hembree Police Station

Monday morning, Olivera got to the office at the usual time and stopped by the kitchenette to say hello to Springer and Reagan, who were helping themselves to coffee and donuts. "Good morning, men."

"Morning, Chief. How 'bout them Hogs!" Springer said, at which a big whoop went up.

"Didn't catch the game, but I'm assuming they won." He set his briefcase on the counter and walked back to Ms. Hill's desk to pick up the mail.

"Course they won, Lieutenant," Reagan said. "Was there ever any doubt?"

"You didn't miss much," Springer said with a chortle. "It was clear where it was going by the end of the first quarter. By the way, Chief, I just took a call for you, Mosey Frye."

"What'd *she* want?"

"I put it in a note. It's on your desk."

"Thanks, I'll give her a call." Olivera filled his cup and headed to his cubicle but stopped and turned back to Springer. "Then let's get started on the Ashby files, get the evidence catalogued and put away."

"Sure thing, Chief, whenever you're ready."

He entered his cubicle, hung up his hat, and slipped

off his sports jacket. Springer's note was stuck to his desk pad. He picked it up and read. "Mosey Frye wants to know when the court intends to release the Eldridge property—house and car. Call cell, please." He fished in his pocket for his phone and called Ms. Frye, whom he'd had on speed dial since the Larkspur incident. "Ms. Frye?" He settled into his chair.

"Lieutenant, thanks for returning my call. Sergeant Springer give you my message?"

"He did, and, it's my understanding that'll happen within the week. I suppose Dr. Wilson has reached a decision?"

"She seems to be shying away from Sunny Banks, but John Earle wanted me to check on it for Martin Sr."

"Yeah, he seemed anxious about it."

"You spoke to him, then?"

"I did, and thanks for the tip. The conversation was helpful, *very* helpful."

"Glad to hear it," Mosey said. "You know there was one thing I didn't mention before, didn't seem that important."

"What's that?"

"Lauren Wilson…"

"What about her?"

"She knew Charles Ashby. Well, knew him. I don't know I'd say she *knew* him, but she'd met him."

"Hmm…didn't know that."

"She said he was the one who told her about Sunny Banks—not specifically, but told her about properties on the outskirts of Hembree. They met when she was here for her interview, back in June."

"Did you fill her in on what happened?"

"I was going to, but she already knew. Said she read

about it on the web."

"That was it, then? She met Ashby, he mentioned properties on the outskirts of town—?"

"I think there was a little more to it than that, Lieutenant, but I wouldn't want to talk out of school. You might give her a call, or better, speak to her in person. She'll be here as soon as she can get away. She's buying another house and wants to get started on the remodel."

"I tell you what," he said. "Ask her to give me a call, please, ma'am."

"Sure, I'll drop her a text."

He had little time to wait before the call came through. In fact, he was on his way to the morgue that afternoon when his cellphone rang. "Lieutenant Olivera here."

"Hi, this is Lauren Wilson."

"Dr. Wilson, thanks for calling. I'm tying up some loose ends in the Ashby case and understand you had contact with the victim back in June. Is that correct?"

"That's right, I met him at the Tavernette when I was in Hembree for my interview."

"How did you happen to meet him?"

"He was in the bar the last night I was there."

"Did he approach you?"

"Yes, he was friendly, welcoming. He seemed to know who I was."

"And how would he know that?"

"I don't know. Maybe the college posted the on-campus interview. Some do."

"Did he mention Sunny Banks specifically?"

"No, but he seemed to be interested in properties in that area, as opposed to the Historic District."

"Huh. Did he say why?"

"Not really, but I thought it a little strange."

"Strange?"

"Yes, I don't know if Mosey mentioned I'm a forensic psychologist. I've had some training in profiling, and I suppose, once I read about the case, Charles's behavior that evening started to make more sense."

"This sounds like a conversation I'd prefer to have in person, if you don't mind. I understand you're coming to Hembree soon?"

"Yes, I'm driving down…leaving in the morning. It'll take a good two days. We could meet on Thursday if that's convenient."

"Thursday's fine. Will you be staying at the Tavernette again?"

"I will."

"Would you mind giving me a call when you get here?"

"Yes, of course."

"Have a safe trip." He clicked off.

Chapter Thirty-Three

Thursday, November 19, 3:00 p.m.
Tavernette

In the Tavernette bar, at three o'clock on a Thursday afternoon, Olivera pulled out a chair for Dr. Lauren Wilson. "Did you have a good trip?"

"I did," she said. "Actually, I prefer to drive. I covered a lot of country I hadn't seen before."

He glanced around at the empty tables. "We should be able to talk in here. Unlikely it'll fill up before happy hour."

She sat and folded her hands in her lap, then scanned the room, chock full of Civil War memorabilia—a big canon, old photographs of battle scenes, Confederate uniforms and caps, and a few old guns and swords.

"What do you want to drink?" he asked.

"A beer would be nice, if you'll join me."

"Sure."

"I'll take an India Pale Ale," she said, "if they have it."

He waved to the bartender. "Could we get a couple of beers?" He placed the order and turned back to Wilson. "Ms. Frye says you've been following the case."

"That's right," she said. "I suppose you could say I have a professional—or maybe morbid—interest in such things, but this time, of course, it was more than that.

First time I've been present at the actual discovery of a body—I mean unprofessionally."

"And if you'd *seen* the body," he said, "we would have been spared some time."

"I know. Sorry about that, but Mosey—"

"Yes, I remember, wouldn't let you near it. Well, no use talking about that. I understand you met Charles Ashby when you were here in June?"

"I did. Right in here, as a matter of fact. I was sitting over there." She nodded toward the bar.

The bartender arrived with their order. "Anything else, Lieutenant?" He set the drinks on the table.

"No, that's all, thanks." Olivera placed a twenty on the tray. "Keep the change." He turned back to Wilson. "You were saying?"

"I was sitting at the bar. I saw him come in with someone, another man. They took a table, then later when his friend left, he approached the bar, ordered a drink, and said something to me, like, 'Enjoying your visit?' I said I was, and he asked if he could join me. He seemed okay to me. I thought maybe I'd seen him earlier on campus. So, he sat down on the next stool, and we started talking."

"Well, that sounds fairly normal. When did things get strange? You said that, right?—that things got a little strange?"

"Yes, maybe 'interesting' would be a better descriptor."

"How so?"

"He began to fit a type—to me, he did."

"Type?" Olivera took a sip of beer.

"He didn't seem genuine. He seemed...anxious to create an impression."

"And did he?"

"Not the impression he was going for."

"Which was?"

"I'd say of someone who was successful, practiced, well-connected."

"So, you think he wasn't any of that?"

"A wanna-be, but, no, he was trying too hard. And after he'd been drinking for a while, he became rather glib. Not interesting at all as a conversationalist. But as a subject—"

"I see," he broke in, "you were profiling him."

She raised her brow and pursed her lips. "I was. A little intrusive, I suppose."

He couldn't help but wonder if she was profiling *him*. He cleared his throat. "What did you conclude?"

"Narcissistic, at least that…an opportunist, if I had to guess. Maybe even a sociopath, but that's a stretch."

"You're good." Olivera's brows shot up.

She looked down at the table.

"Don't be bashful about it," he said. "This profile of yours is very helpful. It fits well with what I've been told by another source."

She looked up. "Johnny Eldridge, you mean."

"That's right." He smiled. "Given your impression of Ashby, you think it fits with what Eldridge claimed?"

She nodded.

Olivera sipped his beer.

"Do you mind if I ask you a question?" she said.

"Go ahead."

"Isn't this all a little anticlimactic? Ashby's dead as a result of what you've determined to be an accident, sounds like. Eldridge won't be charged, will he?"

"Not in Ashby's death. Of course, failure to report

could get a person one to five, but Johnny did attempt to render aid, and the physical evidence corroborated his story."

"I see," she said.

"But the prosecutor's office in Vicksburg might be interested in what you have to say. Would you mind if I let them know?"

"No. I suppose I might as well get started. I expect I'll be called on regularly—in an official capacity."

"Yes, indeed," Olivera said. "Welcome to Hembree, Dr. Wilson."

She smiled, and they clicked glasses.

Poor Springer. First Eads McGinnis and now this one. He laughed, couldn't help himself.

"What's so funny, Lieutenant?"

"Nothing." He shook his head, stared up at the ceiling, and laughed again.

A word about the author...

Kay Pritchett was born and bred in Greenville, Mississippi and attended Millsaps College in Jackson. She completed her education at the University of North Carolina, Chapel Hill, where she received her doctorate in Spanish Literature. After a long stint in Spain, she accepted an offer at the University of Arkansas and, at retirement in 2016, delved fully into fiction writing. *The Incident at Sunny Banks*, inspired by childhood memories of the Delta, is the fifth novel in her Mosey Frye Mysteries series. She lives in Fayetteville, Arkansas, with her husband Christopher J. Huggard.

Thank you for purchasing
this publication of The Wild Rose Press, Inc.

For questions or more information
contact us at
info@thewildrosepress.com.

The Wild Rose Press, Inc.
www.thewildrosepress.com

www.ingramcontent.com/pod-product-compliance
Lightning Source LLC
Chambersburg PA
CBHW051639260626
47170CB00004B/1250